Black
and
Blue
Magic

ZILPHA KEATLEY SNYDER

DRAWINGS BY GENE HOLTAN

A Yearling Book

Published by
Dell Publishing
a division of
The Bantam Doubleday Dell Publishing Group, Inc.
1 Dag Hammarskjold Plaza
New York, New York 10017

Especially for Douglas

Copyright © 1966 by Zilpha Keatley Snyder

All rights reserved. No part of this book may be reproduced or transmitted in any form or by any means, electronic or mechanical, including photocopying, recording, or by any information storage and retrieval system, without the written permission of the Publisher, except where permitted by law.

For information address: Macmillan Publishing Company on behalf of Atheneum Publishers, New York, New York.
Yearling ® TM 913705, Dell Publishing, a division of the Bantam Doubleday Dell Publishing Group, Inc.

ISBN: 0-440-40053-8

Reprinted by arrangement with Macmillan Publishing Company on behalf of Atheneum Publishers

Printed in the United States of America

May 1988

10 9 8 7 6 5 4 3 2 1

CW

OTHER YEARLING BOOKS YOU WILL ENJOY:

THE HEADLESS CUPID, *Zilpha Keatley Snyder*
BLAIR'S NIGHTMARE, *Zilpha Keatley Snyder*
THE FAMOUS STANLEY KIDNAPPING CASE, *Zilpha Keatley Snyder*
THE CHANGELING, *Zilpha Keatley Snyder*
THE EGYPT GAME, *Zilpha Keatley Snyder*
THE TRUTH ABOUT STONE HOLLOW, *Zilpha Keatley Snyder*
THE WITCHES OF WORM, *Zilpha Keatley Snyder*
FATHER'S ARCANE DAUGHTER, *E. L. Konigsburg*
FROM THE MIXED-UP FILES OF MRS. BASIL E. FRANKWEILER, *E. L. Konigsburg*
JENNIFER, HECATE, MACBETH, WILLIAM MCKINLEY, AND ME, ELIZABETH, *E. L. Konigsburg*

YEARLING BOOKS/YOUNG YEARLINGS/YEARLING CLASSICS are designed especially to entertain and enlighten young people. Charles F. Reasoner, Professor Emeritus of Children's Literature and Reading, New York University, is consultant to this series.

For a complete listing of all Yearling titles,
write to Dell Readers Service,
P.O. Box 1045, South Holland, Illinois 60473.

Contents

Black
and
Blue
Magic

Possibilities

On the very first morning of the summer vacation when Harry Houdini Marco was almost twelve years old, a pretty weird thing happened. Right at the time Harry didn't think too much about it, for some reason; maybe because he'd never been the kind of kid who went in for any sort of magic stuff. It wasn't until afterwards that he began to have second thoughts about what happened that day in the attic. But afterwards—considering the way the rest of the summer turned out—he decided he might as well believe there'd been something fishy about that first morning, too.

The day started out badly—about as bad as a first day of vacation possibly could. Harry's first chore was to mow the lawn in front of the boarding house, and it was right then that things started off on the wrong foot. Actually, Harry was feeling cheerful enough when he started, but, right smack dab in the middle of the mowing, a moving van pulled up in front of Pete Wilson's apartment a few doors down Kerry Street. Of course, Harry had known that the Wilsons were planning to move, but he *had* hoped it wouldn't be until the end of the summer. But no such luck. So there went Pete—not one of Harry's best friends but certainly the very last kid anywhere near Harry's age on the whole street. Moving to the suburbs, just like all the families in the neighborhood except the Marcos. Summer vacation suddenly began to look like a long lonely stretch of nothing.

Harry worked off a little bitterness by fiercely mowing down the last surviving column of tall green grass, and then he collapsed, feeling a lot like a mowed-down last survivor himself. But lying there in the sunshine—strangely warm weather for San Francisco in June—he began to feel just a bit better. The air around him was juicy with the damp green smell of cut grass, the sky was blue, and a whole three months of freedom stretched ahead. It looked as if something would almost have to happen.

He propped his heels up on the wheel of the lawn mower and began to consider the possibilities. Maybe somebody really interesting would move into Marco's Boarding House. Of course, there already was Mr. Brighton, except that he was so busy most of the time.

Even better, maybe Mike Wong would come to spend the whole summer with his grandparents at their grocery store on the corner. A whole summer of Mike would really liven things up.

Or it might even be possible that this year Mom would scrape together enough money for a vacation trip. That would be best of all. Every summer for years they'd talked about a trip, but every time it had fallen through. Of course, that wasn't Mom's fault. It takes a lot of money to go on a trip when, on top of all the other expenses, you have to pay someone to run a boarding house while you're gone.

But things had been better than usual at Marco's lately. There had been four steady boarders for quite a while now; and the two little rooms for temporary people had been rented fairly often by traveling salesmen. Yes, the Marcos just might make it this summer—if only the washing machine didn't go on the fritz again, or the furnace blow up, or some other dumb thing happen, as it always seemed to do just when they got a little ahead.

Thinking about all the things that could go wrong was bringing on a relapse of serious gloominess, when Mom came out on the veranda with a dust mop. "Well, if it isn't Hard-Working Harry," she said as she shook the mop over the railing. "I wondered what happened to you when I heard the mower stop half an hour ago. I was afraid you'd disappeared in a puff of smoke, but I see you only collapsed."

Mom hitched herself up onto the porch railing, pulled the old red kerchief off her head and ran her fingers through her curly brown hair. Sitting there on the veranda railing, swinging her legs, and sort of squinting from the sunshine on her face, she almost looked like a—well, like a girl, or something. Harry frowned. As a rule, he never thought much about how Mom looked. But now, he wished she'd get down off the railing and quit wrinkling up her nose that way. After all, a woman with an almost grown-up son—twelve years old in October—oughtn't to go around looking like a teenager, for Pete Squeaks!

After a minute or two, Mom slid down off the railing and started tying the kerchief over her hair. "I can't really blame you," she said. "That sun feels marvelous, after all the fog. But there is a lot to be done. When you finish recuperating from mowing that vast expanse of lawn, there are still the wastebaskets and the garbage, and that broken chair should go up to the attic till I can find the time to fix it. Oh yes, and Miss Thurgood wants you to go to the drugstore for her." Mom looked up at the sunny sky, sighed, and took her dust mop back inside the dark old house.

Harry sat up and scratched his ankles slowly, while he gave his mushy muscles a chance to get used to the idea of getting back to work. That part about the "vast expanse of lawn" had been kidding, of course. Mom was like that; kidding him into getting back to work instead of bawling him out the way some mothers would have done. Actually the lawn was so little that Harry was always scraping himself on something when he tried to turn the mower around to head back the other way.

Really, it was pretty silly to bother with such a dinky patch of grass. Harry had told Mom so more than once. But Mom said it was the only bit of green left on the block, and besides she could remember when she used to play games there when she was a little girl. Of course, things had been different then, and the lawn had been much bigger.

A lot of things had been different back in the old days when Mom was a girl. She had been Lorna Bainbridge before she was married, and the house had been Bainbridge Place, instead of Marco's Boarding House. There'd been lots of big old houses on the block then, and lawns and trees too. But times had changed, and where the big side yard had been, there was now a two-story cement building, squeezed in between Marco's and Wong's Grocery. Where Mom had once played tag on a green lawn, Jason's Cleaners steamed and hissed on the ground floor, and upstairs, Madelaine's School of Ballet tinkled and thumped.

Mr. Jason, the cleaner, wasn't much of a neighbor. He lived some place else, and at his shop he only worked, with no time for visiting. Madelaine was a little more interesting. She was a phony French lady from Chicago, and she lived right there in a little room at the back of the studio. Her ponytail was long and straight and skinny, and so was the rest of her. She looked even more so because of the things she wore—long underwear in bright colors. Mom said the underwear things were called leotards; and Mr. Brighton, who had lots of funny sayings, said that Madelaine had a shape like a yard of pump-water.

Anyway, even before Mom was born, the depression had started things changing, and now all but two of the big old homes were gone: Marco's, and the house right next door where the Furdells lived. And even the Furdells' house could hardly be counted, because a big brick and plaster building had been stuck right on the front of it, where Mrs. Olive Furdell made her candy and sold it.

Harry had scratched both ankles thoroughly, and retied one shoe, since he had first thought about getting up off the grass. There didn't seem to be anything else that needed doing, so he pulled himself together and stood up. The lawn mower, groaning and growling behind him as he pulled it slowly around back to put it away, seemed like an echo of his state of mind.

Usually Harry disliked the job of emptying the garbage and all the wastepaper baskets for the big boarding house, but today he was so busy brooding over his lack of prospects for the summer that he hardly noticed. But the next job, carrying a heavy rocking chair up three flights of stairs to the attic, was hard enough work to force him to give it his full attention. Even with his mind on his work, Harry managed to whack himself on the shins several times and trip himself once, when one of the rockers got stuck between two balusters on the staircase. Harry was too used to that sort of thing to get excited over it, but it did deepen his gloom a little.

Once inside the small fourth-floor attic, Harry cleared a space for the broken chair and then looked around for a place to catch his breath for a minute. A fat round of rolled-up rug looked fairly comfortable, and he collapsed on it on his stomach like a panther lying along a limb of a tree. It was while he was lying there in the warm, dimly lit attic, that the weird thing started happening.

He'd been lying there for a while with his chin on his hands, when his glance happened to wander into a dark corner—and he almost fell right off the rug. There, only a few feet away, a strange, white face was staring at him over the top of a marble-topped washstand. Harry's heart had time for only a couple of fancy beats

before he realized what it really was that he was seeing. Someone had put one of Dad's posters of the old Swami behind the washstand so that just the face stuck out over the top. Harry hadn't actually been frightened, but he couldn't help grinning a little in relief.

Now that he knew what it was, Harry remembered seeing the poster before. It was a phony-looking, old-fashioned picture of the Swami in fancy oriental robes and huge red turban. There were some big black letters across his middle that said THE GREAT SWAMI, but those were now out of sight behind the washstand. All that you could see was the pale wrinkled face, faded and dusty; and two huge dark eyes that for some reason seemed as bright as ever, so that they seemed to blaze out at you from the dim corner.

The poster had belonged to Dad way back when he was a boy. Even way back then Dad had planned on a career as a magician, and the old Swami, along with Harry Houdini and all the other famous magicians, had been his idols. Dad had turned out to be a magician all right, and when Harry was born Dad had named him after Harry Houdini—which at least was better than being named after the Swami—and Harry was supposed to grow up to be the greatest magician of all. Only, for some reason, Harry had never been able to fit himself into Dad's plans.

Harry was just lying there thinking about things like that, and wondering how he happened to turn out to be such an unmagical type, when all at once the Swami winked one of his big black eyes. For the next few seconds Harry was too astonished to think about anything, and before he could get his wits about him, the poster face smiled, with a hundred little rearrangements of wrinkles and a gleam of white teeth. A cracked and creaky voice that Harry remembered hearing once before said, "Remarkable weather we're having, isn't it?"

It was the usual kind of thing for people to say when it was warm in San Francisco in the summertime, but it was pretty unusual for a poster to say it. Harry had a little trouble getting his voice started when he said, "Yes, sir. Yes, it is."

The poster face turned a bit and seemed to sniff the air. "Invigorating," the creaky voice went on. "The air is absolutely heavy with possibilities. Don't you agree?"

"Well, I . . . that is . . . I guess I hadn't noticed," Harry managed to say.

The Swami's painted eyes focused sharply on Harry and he frowned. "Oh, but you must," he said sharply.

"You can't afford not to notice. Possibilities are easily missed. Possibilities are . . ."

Just about then Harry's chin slipped off his hands with a jerk, he blinked, and the poster face was suddenly stiff and silent above the marble top of the washstand. Without taking his eyes off the Swami's face for an instant, Harry got to a sitting position, and then slowly stood up. But the face in the dark corner stayed flat and faded even when Harry climbed over some stacked-up boxes, leaned across the washstand, and ran his fingers over the faded dusty surface.

Harry went back to the rolled-up rug and sat down to think. That's when he decided the whole thing must have been a dream. Of course, it had seemed awfully real and there *was* the fact that Harry almost never went to sleep in the daytime; but what other answer *could* there be. He stretched out on the rug again just to see how it would be for sleeping and, sure enough, it was soft and comfortable, and there was something very drowsy about the warm and slightly stuffy attic air.

Harry breathed a sigh of relief. That was it, of course. He'd gone to sleep looking at the poster and was dreaming until his chin slipping off his hands woke him up. Right at that moment, Harry was positive he'd found the answer, but just the same he couldn't help turning around quickly to grab a sneaking glance at the poster just before he went out the attic door.

He was still thinking about the dream as he went looking for Mom so as to get the money and prescription for Miss Thurgood's medicine. He found her on her knees scrubbing the tub in the second-floor bathroom.

The water splashing into the tub was making a lot of noise, so he just leaned against the door frame and waited, admiring the quick, efficient way Mom did the scrubbing. She did everything that way; fast, and with no waste motion. With a mother like that, and a father who had been a magician, with all the "hand is quicker than the eye" stuff, you'd think a guy would just naturally be well co-ordinated. You'd think he'd have extra good control of his hands and feet, instead of being the kind who usually couldn't make it to first base without falling all over himself. The kind who gets nicknamed things like Cement Hands, or Humpty Dumpty Harry.

Of course Mr. Brighton, who knew a lot about sports and things, said that Harry was big and strong, and once he quit growing so fast he'd probably stop being so clumsy. But it didn't look too hopeful. Here he was almost twelve years old, and things didn't seem to be improving very fast.

Mom sighed, sat back on her heels, and ran the back of her hand across her forehead. She turned off the water and stood up before she noticed Harry. "Well, hi!" she said. When she smiled, she didn't look so tired any more.

"Hi," Harry said. "I'm all through except going to the drugstore for Miss Thurgood."

"Oh, my goodness," Mom said, digging into her pocket for the money and prescription. "I'm glad you remembered. I was thinking about something else so hard I'd almost forgotten about it." As Harry started to leave, she went on. "I'm almost afraid to mention it, but you know what I've been thinking about? I've been wondering if maybe we'd finally be able to take that trip this summer. If we can just keep our steady boarders, and nothing expensive needs fixing, it looks as if we ought to be able to make it this time. At least for a week or two."

"Hey!" Harry said, forgetting all about everything else; gloomy moods and crazy dreams included, "That's great. Do you suppose we could go out in the country somewhere? Like on one of those farms or ranches that take boarders, sort of. What do they call those places?"

"I guess they're called guest ranches," Mom said. "We can look into it, I suppose, if you're sure that's what you want to do. I've heard those places are pretty expensive, but it won't hurt to inquire. Maybe we can find one that's not too expensive."

Harry made like a cowboy riding a horse and swinging a lasso over his head. "Yippee!" he yelled.

Mom laughed. "Now don't go getting your hopes up too high," she warned. "You know how quickly things can go wrong around here. We mustn't really count on it. But it does begin to look like a possibility."

Harry had started out the door but that turned him around with a jerk. "Did you say a . . . possibility?" he asked.

As Harry got out his old bike for the trip to the drugstore he was thinking it was too bad Mom happened to use that particular phrase. And just when he'd gotten the whole thing nicely settled in his mind, too. Of course, he was still positive that it had all been a dream. But you couldn't help wondering about things like—possibilities!

The Medicine Mess

By the time Harry got to Brown's Drugs and Notions, he'd quit worrying about possibilities and was busy planning his two weeks on a guest ranch. In fact he was so busy he didn't even take time out to look over the selection of new funny books while he waited for Mr. Brown to fill the prescription.

Ordinarily, the funny book situation was the only good thing about having Miss Thurgood as a boarder. Mr. Brown was touchy about people who came in his store just to read the funny books. Sometimes he even made sarcastic comments in a loud voice about not running a lending library. But he didn't mind at all if an actual customer picked up something to browse through while he waited for a prescription to be filled. Miss Thurgood took just about enough medicine to keep Harry up-to-date on his favorite funny book characters.

But today he had other things to think about. For years Harry had wanted to live in the country. He had a favorite daydream about how he'd get a lot of money somehow—by winning a contest or getting a reward for some brave deed—and then he'd buy a ranch way out in the country. That way, he'd have the kind of life he wanted, and Mom wouldn't have to work so hard running a boarding house to make a living. Of course, two weeks wouldn't be as good as really living in the country, but it would be great while it lasted.

"Here you are, Harry," Mr. Brown said. "That will be three dollars and seventy-five cents." This time Miss Thurgood's medicine was red and syrupy and came in a great big bottle. It wouldn't fit in any of Harry's pockets so it would have to ride home in the bicycle basket. That meant that Harry had better get his mind off the country and put it very firmly on what he was doing. The last time he brought Miss Thurgood's medicine home in the bike basket something awful had happened. He'd forgotten the bottle of pills and ridden right over a curb with a big thump, and the bottle had flown out and smashed all over the street. At least it *had* been pills that time so Harry was able to find most of them and take them home in his pocket; but Miss Thurgood hadn't been very happy about her pills being "rolled around a dirty street and then stuffed into a *boy's* pocket." Miss Thurgood always said the word "boy" in a slightly disgusted tone of voice.

This time Harry rode very carefully and missed all the bumps, and the medicine was still all right when he came in the back door and put it on the kitchen table. Mom was working at the sink. They'd just started a very interesting discussion about how soon Mom was going to get around to writing letters to the guest ranch places, when Miss Thurgood's screechy voice called from upstairs.

"Oh dear," Mom said. "You'd better run up and take her medicine to her. She seems to be in a big hurry for it. She's called down three times to see if you were back from the drugstore."

Miss Thurgood was standing at the head of the stairs looking very impatient. When she saw Harry she said, "At last!" and shut her mouth firmly. When she felt like it, Miss Thurgood could close her mouth in a way that always made Harry expect to hear a clanking noise. Besides that, she could make her eyebrows come down almost to her nose. Harry never could understand how she could do that when her hair was pulled back so tight into the bun on the back of her head. Miss Thurgood's hairdo was one of the things Mr. Brighton had a saying about. He said with a hairdo like that one, you'd have to stand on your tiptoes to spit.

But Miss Thurgood was a good reliable boarder, and they were hard to come by, so it was important to keep her happy. Harry decided to run up the stairs to make it look as if he'd really been hurrying. It would have been a good idea, too, if anybody else had had it. Anybody except Humpty Harry—the World's Clumsiest Kid.

He was almost to the top of the stairs when all of a sudden one of his feet didn't get out of the way of the other one, and the next thing he knew his elbow hit the top stair with a crash that knocked the bottle of medicine right out of his hand. The next few minutes were almost too painful to talk about, in more ways than one.

Dinner time that night was pretty grim, too. Miss Thurgood kept having coughing spells behind a lace-trimmed handkerchief, and then explaining, in a gasping

sort of voice, how hard it was for her to keep going without her wonderful medicine.

Mr. Konkel looked concerned, and every time Miss Thurgood disappeared behind her handkerchief for another coughing spell, he would gaze at Harry accusingly. Mrs. Pusey and Mr. Brighton seemed to take it pretty calmly, though.

Mrs. Pusey was a quiet grandmotherly lady, with gray hair and sad eyes. She didn't talk very much, and it was hard to tell what she was thinking. You wouldn't know she was even interested in kids, except that once in a while she brought Harry a doughnut from the bakery shop where she worked.

On the other hand, Mr. Konkel was very interested

in kids—too interested. Mr. Konkel was the kind of person who seemed to feel that it was up to him personally to keep every kid he met from going to absolute rack and ruin. He had a million little lectures about what you should and shouldn't do, and he was always talking about juvenile delinquents and looking at Harry pointedly. He loved to tell little stories about what he did when he was a boy. Some people who do that are pretty interesting, but Mr. Konkel must have been just about the most boring kid who ever lived.

Anyway, Mr. Konkel listened very seriously to Miss Thurgood's story about how Harry had charged up the stairs and hurled the medicine bottle at her left ankle. According to Miss Thurgood it was only because she stepped aside so quickly, that the bottle missed her and smashed on the wall instead. Mr. Konkel kept looking at Harry and nodding his head as if it was just what he'd been expecting all along.

Mom was out in the kitchen when Miss Thurgood told the other boarders her version of the story. So it was up to Harry to set them all straight. But every time he got started Miss Thurgood drowned him out with another coughing fit. So, finally, he just gave up.

He was feeling pretty miserable until he glanced at Mr. Brighton. As soon as he caught Harry's eye, Mr. Brighton gave a wink and a grin that said he thought the whole thing was a big joke. And if you thought it over, it really was funny, except Miss Thurgood might move out; and if she did—there went her room-and-board money. And without Miss Thurgood's room-and-board money—there went the vacation trip.

Mike Wong

The next morning Harry was on his way to Wong's Grocery to get two loaves of bread for Mom when he noticed the sunshine on the porch swing. The early morning sun was slanting onto the veranda making an inviting glow across the padded seat. Two days in a row of early morning sunshine right at the beginning of the vacation. It occurred to Harry right away that such an unusual circumstance ought not to be wasted.

He arranged himself on the warm pillows, being careful not to bump his sore elbow on the back of the swing. The elbow was pretty tender. After he was comfortably settled, and the swing had slowed to a gentle swaying, he twisted the arm around to get a better look. Sure enough, there was an ugly-looking purplish-red spot as big as a silver dollar. Harry examined it with a certain satisfaction. He was an authority on bruises, and this was going to be an impressive one. He thought briefly of showing it to Miss Thurgood to prove he really hadn't thrown the medicine at her on purpose, but on second thought he decided not to bother. He had a feeling that if Miss Thurgood wanted to believe something, there wasn't any use showing her evidence to the contrary.

In a mood of scientific curiosity, Harry decided to test his diagnosis. Lifting his right foot, he pulled up the leg of his jeans. Just as he expected, the bruise on his shin, although larger, didn't have nearly the color and quality of the elbow one. It hadn't hurt as much, either, although it had been just about as embarrassing. It had happened on the Sutter Street bus when he was hurrying to get off. He'd tripped over something—or maybe, over nothing, just as like as not. He'd staggered forward, grabbed a hand hold, spun around and wound up sort of sitting in a fat lady's lap. Afterwards, his shin had begun to hurt, although he couldn't remember bumping it on anything. He had a hunch, though, that the fat lady had kicked him. She'd looked as if she wanted to, anyway.

Examining your wounds is a good way to start feeling sorry for yourself, and it wasn't long before Harry had worked himself up into a very melancholy frame of mind. When you stopped to think it over, what did he have to be happy about? Here he was, probably the clumsiest kid in ten states, practically an orphan—at least, halfway one—living on a crummy old street where there was nothing but shops and stores and grownups. It was enough to give anybody the blues.

When Harry was really in the mood to feel sorry for himself he usually thought about his father. It wasn't just that is father was dead, either. It was sad, of course, that his father had died when Harry was only six years old, but that had been long ago, and time had dimmed the memory. Nowadays, Harry could feel even more miserable by thinking about what a disappointment he would be to Dad if he were still alive.

Harry could still remember just how Dad had looked; tall, and dark and slender—just right for a magician. There was a swift certainty about everything he did, and his hands could move so fast it made you dizzy trying to keep track of them. But most clearly of all, he could remember how Dad had planned and counted on Harry's becoming a great magician, too. Even when Harry was a little tiny kid, Dad used to try to teach him things: like how to handle cards and do tricks with handkerchiefs. Dad always said that Harry's clumsiness was only because he was so young, but Harry could tell he was disappointed.

And then, there had been the time that Dad took him to see the Great Swami. Harry grinned thinking about his crazy dream the day before in the attic. He had to admit he'd been a little scared there for a minute, but not nearly as scared as he'd been the time when he really met the Swami.

By the time Harry was born, the Great Swami was such an old man that he didn't do a stage act any more. But he'd once been famous for mind-reading and foretelling and Dad wanted the old Swami to tell Harry's future. Partly, Harry had been scared because the old man looked like a shriveled up old lizard in a turban, but mostly he'd been afraid of what the Swami might say. He just didn't know how Dad would take it if the Great Swami said that magic was always going to be a problem for Harry.

But strangely enough it had turned out all right.

The old man had stared at Harry a long time and then in a slow, splintery voice he'd said, "The boy has a rare gift, and his magic will be of a very special kind." Harry never had been sure what that meant, but it seemed to make Dad happy. He talked about it a lot and he always called it "The Prophecy." After that he made Harry work even harder with the cards and handkerchiefs.

It really makes a guy feel miserable to think about messing up a prophecy and being a disgrace to a name like Harry Houdini Marco. So, because he was in that sort of a mood, Harry thought about it some more, until he had worked himself into a really colossal case of the blues. He was just doing a quick rerun of his list of troubles to see if he'd forgotten anything, when a familiar voice said, "Hey!"

Harry's carefully constructed castle of gloom exploded as he lurched to his feet with a force that sent the swing thudding back against the wall. "Hey Mike!" he yelled.

Mike Wong had been one of Harry's best friends for years—but only during vacations. That was because Mike really lived in Berkeley. It was only when school was out that he came to spend a few days with his grandparents, who lived in an apartment over their store on the corner of Kerry Street.

Mike was almost exactly Harry's age and just about the same size. But that's where the likeness ended. The difference was that Mike Wong was just about the best athlete that Harry had ever known. Mike could run the fifty yard dash in six and a half seconds, he had a terrific batting eye, and he could pitch a ball that was almost impossible to hit—and right over the plate, too. And in kick ball, he kicked a low hard fly that whistled over fielders' heads like a bullet. He could do it time after time without one goof, and without asking for "bouncies" either.

Mike was standing on the veranda stairs, grinning up at Harry. There was a bat over his shoulder with a mitt stuck on the end of it, and he had a ball in his hand. "Want to go to the park and knock a ball around?" he said.

"Sure," Harry said. "Just a minute till I ask Mom." He was halfway through the door when he remembered about the loaves of bread. "Oops," he said. "Hey, I better run down to your store first. I was supposed to get some bread a long time ago and I sort of forgot about it. I think I'd better get it before I ask about the park, if you know what I mean."

Mike grinned. "Yeah, I know what you mean," he said.

Mike's grandfather, Mr. Williamson Wong, waited on Harry at the store. Mr. and Mrs. Wong were quiet gentle people who gave suckers to little kids and let customers who were having a bad time wait and wait to pay their bills. They'd helped Mom out more than once when the boarding house wasn't doing too well. Except, maybe, for Lee Furdell, they were just about Harry's favorite people on the block.

When Harry and Mike clattered into the kitchen with the bread, Mom was so glad to see Mike again that she didn't say much about how long it had taken Harry to get back. She said it was all right about the park and she even made them some sandwiches to take along.

The bus ride to the park was just about long enough to catch up on all the gossip since Easter, when they'd last seen each other. Harry knew a lot of good places in Golden Gate Park where there was room to bat a ball around, particularly on a weekday when it wasn't so crowded. They found a nice deserted stretch of lawn and had a good time practicing batting and pitching and catching. Harry did a little better than usual and it really made him feel encouraged.

Actually, it wasn't that Harry was so awful at sports; at times he did pretty well. It was more that he was so unreliable. Just when he'd been doing fine, he was sure to fall on his face—or flat on his back, like the time he'd stepped on a ball he was trying to kick. But he always tried, at least.

Once, a long time ago, Mike had said, "The thing about you, Harry, is you've got guts. You never chicken out, no matter how much you goof up."

That was one of the nicest things anybody had ever said about Harry. But that was the way Mike was. Even though he was so great at everything, he never gloated, like some hot-shot types. And he always said some little thing to make you feel better. Even if it was just, "Nice try," or "Tough luck."

That day at the park started out to be terrific. Late in the afternoon a bunch of big guys, about fourteen years old, let Harry and Mike join their game and it was great to watch their eyes bug out when they saw what Mike could do. And Harry wasn't so bad himself. He hit a couple of Mike's pitches and caught a sizzling line drive without even spraining a finger. It would have been a neat day except for one thing.

They were resting under a tree before starting off for home, when something happened that spoiled everything. They'd been talking about how great it was that summer vacation had started and Harry said, "Hey, why don't you see if you can spend a lot of time at your grandparents' this summer? Maybe a whole month or two. We could have a lot of fun. We could go to the zoo and Playland and come here to the park." He broke off noticing the funny expression on Mike's face.

"It sounds great," Mike said, "but I guess I can't. My dad's got a summer coaching job at this old camp up in the Sierras. Mom and I are going with him, and we'll be gone almost till school starts."

So there went one of Harry's best plans for the summer. Poof! Just like that—the way his Dad used to make a fish bowl disappear in a puff of smoke.

Harry to the Rescue

On the way home from Golden Gate Park in the bus, Mike kept bringing up good things to talk about; like how the Giants were doing; and this spooky TV show, about a huge bloodshot eye that came down from Mars and crawled around like a spider. But Harry had a hard time keeping his mind on the conversation. He was feeling too disappointed—and jealous.

He kept thinking that some people sure were lucky. Mike's father was a high school coach in Oakland; so, no wonder Mike was so terrific at sports. And if that wasn't lucky enough, now Mike was going to get to spend a whole summer in the Sierras. Mike had tried to make it sound as if it weren't anything great so Harry wouldn't feel bad, but that didn't fool Harry. There'd probably be swimming and all sorts of other sports, and maybe even horseback riding every single day. Harry sighed.

Mike went on chattering away and Harry mostly just sat there staring straight ahead. They were in their favorite seat, at the very back of the bus, and there wasn't anyone else in the whole back part except one funny little man. Harry noticed the man because he had a dusty out-of-date look about him and his hair stuck out in a funny way around the brim of his hat. He kept fidgeting all the time and looking at a big old pocket watch. He'd hold up the watch and then glance out of the window, and then he'd look under the seat where there was a great big suitcase that stuck out into the aisle.

Harry was just thinking, rather bitterly, that he'd be sure to fall over that suitcase if it was still there when they got to Kerry Street, when, suddenly the little man leaped to his feet. The bus had pulled to a stop and some people were getting on at the front door. The man grabbed frantically at his suitcase and started to leave, but it was jammed under the seat so tightly that it didn't come loose. Then when it finally did come loose, it came so suddenly that the little man staggered backward. By the time he got going forward again the door was starting to close. The little guy lurched through and made it to the sidewalk, but the suitcase wasn't so lucky. In the rush, it hadn't gotten turned around endways so, of course, it got stuck in the door. When the suitcase stopped coming, the little man's feet flew up and he sat down quickly on the sidewalk. The bus doors finished shutting and as the bus moved slowly forward, the suitcase just slid down into the step well and stayed there.

Afterwards, Harry couldn't imagine what had gotten into him. It really wasn't any of his business. Maybe it was because he knew what it felt like. Having fallen out of and into so many things himself, he knew too darn well what it felt like. Anyway, he didn't wait to explain it to Mike, who hadn't seen the whole thing, or to tell the driver, who apparently hadn't noticed it at all. Instead he just leaped to his feet, pulled the stop cord, and started tugging the suitcase up out of the step well. It was jammed so tight that he didn't get it loose until the bus had almost reached the next stop.

As he started out the door Mike yelled, "Hey, where are you going?"

"I'm taking this suitcase back to the man who lost it," Harry called back. "Want to come along?"

Mike started to jump up, but then he sat back down again. "I can't," he said. "I haven't any more bus money."

As the bus pulled away, Harry shouted through the window, "So long. See you later—at the store!"

It wasn't until Harry had started back down the sidewalk, staggering a bit under the weight of the suitcase, that it occurred to him that he didn't have any more money for the bus fare either. As he struggled along, setting the suitcase down now and then to rest and change hands, he began to realize that he'd done a pretty stupid thing—as usual. What if the man had hailed a taxi, or caught another bus? It would be impossible to find him. Harry couldn't just go off and leave the suitcase and, just as certainly, he couldn't walk all the way home carrying it. And how would it sound if he tried to explain it to a policeman? "Oh-er, Mr. Policeman. Have you seen a little man in a funny hat? You see, I jumped off a bus with his suitcase and . . ." No, Harry decided, it would be better not to try to explain it to anyone, except as a last resort.

But the suitcase was unbelievably heavy, and Harry had just about decided that he'd reached the last-resort stage, when he saw the little man. He was sitting on a bus bench with his elbows on his knees and his chin in his hands, looking terribly tired and dejected. His face, which Harry really hadn't seen before, was as round and pink as the Gerber Baby, only with wrinkles. But there was no mistaking the old-fashioned hat, or the hair that stuck out in funny little tufts over his ears. He looked so mournful, sitting there staring at the ground, that you couldn't help feeling sorry for him.

He didn't even look up until Harry tapped him on the shoulder. "Excuse me, Mister," Harry said. "I think this suitcase belongs to you."

The man jumped, gasped, and the minute he saw the suitcase he grabbed it and sort of hugged it up onto his lap. "Yes, yes," he said, "my suitcase. It *is* my suitcase. It really is my suitcase! I felt quite sure I'd never see it again. Quite sure. And here it is back again. I don't know how to thank you, young man. Indeed I don't." The suitcase was so big that he had to stretch to look over the top of it, and he kept patting it as he talked, as if to make sure it was really there.

"I saw you lose it on the bus," Harry said. He didn't mention the part about getting stuck in the door and falling down, because he always preferred not to have it mentioned when he did that sort of thing. "So I grabbed it and jumped off the bus as soon as I could, and then I came back this way looking for you."

The little man looked astounded. "You did that?" he said. "You really did? My! My! How very clever of you—and how kind. You really don't know how I appreciate this. You can't imagine how important this case is to me, and how necessary it was for me to get it back before . . . Well, I can only tell you that I would have been in very serious trouble if it had been lost or if it had fallen into the wrong hands." The little man's shoulders twitched in an uncontrollable shudder and for a moment he seemed lost in thought. Not very pleasant thought either, judging by the pained expression on his face.

Then suddenly he seemed to pull himself together. "But that's neither here nor there," he said, crinkling his face into a smile that made him seem, more than ever, like a weather-beaten cherub. With a jerky little bounce, he hitched himself over on the bench to make room for Harry. "You must sit down and rest a moment. I know only too well how tiring it is for a rather small person to carry this heavy case."

Harry was in a hurry to get started for home, but he sat down for a moment to be polite. The stranger was still chattering away. "I am greatly indebted to you. You can't imagine what the loss of my case would have meant. I'm very much afraid it would have been the last straw—the Final Mistake, you might say."

"Final?" Harry asked. The word had such an unpleasant sound.

"Yes, in a sense. At the very least it would have greatly increased my troubles."

"Are you already in trouble, then?" Harry asked.

"Trouble?" The man gave a deep sigh, and his face, for a second, seemed to take on a depth Harry would have thought impossible a moment before. "Is it not trouble that I am a wanderer upon the face of the earth; that I have no place to call my own; that my back is tired and my feet ache; that I must find a place to stay in a new city every few days . . ."

It was at that point that Harry interrupted. He hadn't helped run a boarding house for almost six years for nothing. "Have you a place to stay in San Francisco?" he asked quickly.

31

"I stopped at a small hotel last night. But it was not particularly satisfactory. If it looks as if my business will keep me in the city for a while, I may have to look elsewhere."

"I know just the place for you," Harry said quickly, pulling out his wallet. He always carried a few of his mother's cards for just such occasions. "My mother runs a boarding house on Kerry Street. Nice and quiet and good home-cooking. A lot of traveling salesmen come back to our place every time they're in town."

The man stretched his arm up over the suitcase to take the card. It was a little dirty and beat up, but you could still see that it said:

MARCO'S BOARDING HOUSE
318 Kerry Street
Mrs. Lorna Marco, Proprietress
Quiet—Comfortable—Good Food

"You are a salesman, aren't you?" Harry asked.

The little man gave one of his big sighs. "Yes indeed," he said. "I am a salesman."

"I thought so," Harry said. "I can usually spot a traveling salesman right away, because we have so many of them stay with us. I don't know, though, if I would have guessed about you or not. That is, if we hadn't talked. But I do know something about what you're selling, I'll bet."

"You know what I'm selling?" The man clutched the suitcase against his chest. His eyes peering over the top rounded with horror and then flattened with indignation. "You opened it!" he accused. "What right had you to open my case? You must swear that you will not tell . . ."

"Gee Mister," Harry interrupted. "I didn't open your case. I was just starting to say I knew it sure was heavy, whatever it was. I was just making a joke."

After a moment the man relaxed and sighed with relief. "I see that you are telling the truth. Forgive me. This has been a very trying day and I am not myself." He reached in his pocket and pulled out the funny old watch. "I must be going now. I have an appointment with a possible customer. But I will remember what you have done for me."

From a pocket inside his coat, he brought something out and handed it to Harry. "May I present my card in return," he said. The card was thick and heavy, with a worn and yellowed look about it. The printing was so fancy and so covered with curlicues that it was hard to tell what it said. It wasn't until later, that Harry made out all the letters and decided that it said:

Tarzack Mazzeeck
Representative-at-Large
for the
A. A. Comus Co.

The little man was glancing nervously at his watch again. "I really must hurry along," he said. "But we shall meet again soon. I fear I shall never be able to repay sufficiently the favor you have done me."

"Oh, it wasn't anything," Harry said. "And it was

nice meeting you, Mr. . . . Mr. . . ." He looked down trying to make out the printing on the card in his hand.

"Mazzeeck," the man said. "Tarzack Mazzeeck. Forever at your service." He stood up bracing himself against the weight of the heavy suitcase.

"Well, good-by, Mr. Mazzeeck. Be seeing you."

As Harry started off on the long walk home, he kept thinking about the odd little man. There had been something so unusual about him that it almost seemed now as if he really didn't exist. Harry felt as if the whole thing could have been another silly dream—except of course, this time it hadn't. It *had* really happened and only a few minutes before, too.

Maybe the whole thing had something to do with the air being "heavy with possibilities," Harry thought— not seriously, of course, but just sort of fooling around with the idea. For instance, what if there was a possibility that the guy was a billionaire in disguise and the suitcase had been full of his most valuable business papers. Maybe tomorrow Harry would get a letter with a million dollars reward in it.

It was a great idea, but Harry knew it was a dumb one. For one thing, papers, no matter how valuable, couldn't have weighed that much. And besides, Harry couldn't help feeling that, if the little man really were in disguise, he was hiding something more than the fact that he was just a common billionaire.

Hot Water and Hysterics

Harry walked and walked and walked—past dinner time and sundown and twilight. It was almost dark when his aching feet carried him through the gate and around to the back door of the boarding house. The front door was a few steps closer, but some of the guests were usually in the living room in the evenings; and in case Mom was mad, he'd just as soon give her a chance to bawl him out in the privacy of the kitchen. He was hoping that she wasn't too mad and wondering if she'd saved him any dinner, when he opened the back door and got the shock of his life.

Mom was sitting at the kitchen table with her head in her hands and she was *crying*. Mom never cried—not that Harry ever knew about, anyway. When she heard Harry, she raised her head and started to brush the tears away with the back of her hands.

Harry felt awful. "Hey Mom," he said. "Don't do that. I'm sorry I'm late. It really wasn't my fault."

Mom sniffed and smiled, but the smile wobbled and so did her voice. "Oh, it's not that," she said. "I knew what happened to you. Mike came over and told me. He said he thought you were out of money and would probably have to walk home. It wasn't that at all."

"Well, what was it then? What happened?"

"It was the water heater." Mom took out a handkerchief and blew her nose. "It was the water heater . . and Miss Thurgood," she added in a quavery voice that ended up in a sob and then, all of a sudden, turned into a giggle

Harry was alarmed. It was beginning to look as if Mom was cracking up, right before his eyes. But just about then, Mom quit giggling and started acting like a normal mother again.

"I'm sorry to act so silly, Harry," she said. "But you just can't imagine what's been going on here. Right after dinner I was sitting in the front room talking to Mrs. Pusey. Miss Thurgood had just gone upstairs to take her bath. You know how she is about her bath."

Harry knew Miss Thurgood's baths, all right. She always took them early because she liked to use lots of hot water and soak for a long time. Miss Thurgood's bath was another subject that Harry and Mr. Brighton made up jokes about. Mr. Brighton said he bet she was soaking herself in vinegar, because she was in training to become a pickle.

"Anyway," Mom went on, "all of a sudden she called from the bathroom and said there wasn't any hot water. I called back that I'd check the water heater. You know it hasn't been too reliable lately. When I got to the kitchen, I found the whole floor flooded. The water was about a half inch deep and getting deeper. It was only warm though, so the fire must have gone out some time before. I waded over to the pantry, and sure enough, the whole bottom was out of the water heater, rusted clear through. I knew the thing couldn't last much longer, but I had so hoped it would hold out until after our vacation trip. I was so mad about having to spend some of our trip money on a water heater, and so worried about the water getting out into the hall, that I forgot all about Miss Thurgood. I found the little wheels that shut off the water, and I was just getting out the mop and pail, when Miss Thurgood stormed through the door. She had on that long old wool bathrobe she wears, and she had her bath brush in one hand and her bar of soap in the other. She just had time to say, 'Mrs. Marco! *Where* is my hot water?' when she stepped in it and her feet slid out from under her."

Mom started to giggle again. "She looked so funny sitting there in the water, with her bath brush still in her hand like a scepter, or something, that I . . . it was awful of me, but I just couldn't help it . . . I started to laugh."

By now Harry was laughing, too. "But that wasn't all," Mom said between snorts and splutters. "I said something, too. I said, 'You're sitting in it.' " At that

Harry and Mom both broke down and laughed until they were weak.

After a while Mom sobered down and wiped her eyes. "It's really not so funny, though," she said. "Miss Thurgood has gone. She dripped right up to her room and packed a bag and left. She said she'd been insulted and that she'd send for the rest of her things tomorrow. So after she'd gone and I'd finished mopping up the floor, I sat down here and started thinking about how I'd ruined our chances for a trip, after I've been promising you one since you were seven. We might have managed a short trip, even with a new water heater to buy, but with Miss Thurgood's leaving . . ." Mom shook her head sadly.

"Look, Mom," Harry said. "Don't worry about it. I've got plenty of things to do this summer. As a matter of fact, a trip might interfere with some of my other plans." Of course, that was a big fat lie, if there ever was one; but Harry said it so convincingly, that for a moment he almost believed it himself. The realization that the last of his summer plans had fizzled was just beginning to take hold of him when Mr. Brighton came in.

The kitchen door swung open, and Mr. Brighton's head appeared. "Well," he said, "if it isn't Mr. Harry Marco in conference with his chief assistant." Mr. Brighton was always kidding Harry about running the boarding house. He made a big joke out of it most of the time, but once Harry had overheard him telling Mom what a great job she'd done raising Harry. Mr. Brighton had said it was unusual and refreshing to meet a kid who shouldered responsibility so cheerfully.

Mom had said, "I know. Sometimes I worry that it's too much responsibility. But when I started the boarding house I had so much to learn, and Harry just seemed to learn right along with me."

"That's what I get such a kick out of," Mr. Brighton said. "Sometimes I think he knows more about running a boarding house than you do."

So Harry knew what Mr. Brighton really meant by that sort of kidding. But right now, Mr. Brighton didn't say any more about Mr. Harry Marco's boarding house. He seemed to have something else on his mind. He pulled out a chair and sat down. "I was wondering if there's any coffee available down here," he said. Harry got a cup and Mom poured some coffee from the percolator that she always kept filled on the kitchen table. "But to tell the truth, I'm also just curious. A little while ago I looked out my door to see if Miss Thurgood had finished marinating in the bathroom, and I was just in time to see her come stomping out of her room all dressed up and carrying a suitcase. Is anything up?" He grinned at Harry. "You been throwing any more medicine bottles lately?"

"No," Mom said. "I'm afraid I'm the guilty party this time, and I'm awfully afraid she's gone for good." Mom got up to get Harry a plate of food she'd kept for him in the warming oven, and then she sat back down again and told the whole story over for Mr. Brighton. Mom and Harry got hysterical all over again, and when she finished the three of them just sat there and laughed like a bunch of idiots.

The Marriage Plan

It was while the three of them, Harry and Mom and Mr. Brighton, were together there in the kitchen, that Harry started his Plan. It really wasn't a plan at first, just the ghost of an idea; but that night in his third-floor room, he thought about it some more.

Sitting cross-legged on the foot of his bed, he could look right out of the window and across the bay. He often sat there when he had something special to think about. Sometimes the fog drifted in from the Golden Gate and rose higher and higher, drowning the city noise and glare in cool gray mist.

Harry liked it up there on the third floor. It was just a tiny place that was supposed to be a servant's room; but it was separate and private, and its little gabled window had the best view in the house. If he leaned right out, he could even see part of the downtown sky line right on the other side of Madelaine's clothesline and T.V. antenna. It had been his own idea to give up his big bedroom on the second floor. That way, they could take an extra boarder and, besides, he liked the third floor best.

That night, as he enjoyed his own private view, his idea began to form into a real plan. There were a lot of little things from which the Plan grew. First, there had been the other day when it had occurred to him that Mom was pretty young looking, and sort of cute, too. Then tonight, there'd been the way they'd all laughed together around the kitchen table. And part of the Plan was, of course, because of Mr. Brighton and the way he was.

Mr. Brighton was just about the best boarder that Marco's had ever had. He was a big tall man with curly grayish hair. He had a great sense of humor and he liked to talk about interesting things, like sports and animals. In fact, Mr. Brighton owned a farm. Well, it wasn't exactly a farm, but it was a place in the country, up in Marin County. It was a big old farmhouse with a barn and a small pasture. Before his wife died, Mr. Brighton had lived there and commuted into the city every day, and they'd had horses and all sorts of other pets. The farm was rented now, but once when Mr. Brighton had to go there to see about fixing something, he'd taken Harry with him. It really was a neat place.

The farm was one of the most interesting things about Mr. Brighton, but besides that he had a swell job. He managed a sporting-goods store on Market Street— everything from skis to bowling balls. Harry sometimes dropped in there for a visit when he was downtown, and Mr. Brighton always took time out to be friendly and show him around.

In the kitchen, Harry had just happened to think it was too bad that Mr. Brighton and his wife hadn't had any children, because he would have been a neat father. And that thought led to some others.

Mom had had some boy friends in the years since Dad died. Even Mr. Konkel had taken her to the movies once or twice, and bought her candy and stuff like that. But Harry could tell that Mom didn't like any of them very much. Particularly Mr. Konkel.

He'd never really thought about Mom's ever marrying anybody—or if it had occurred to him, he hadn't much liked the idea. But if you gave it some fair and unprejudiced consideration, you had to admit that having a stepfather might not be so bad after all. For one thing, Mom wouldn't have to work so hard, and for another, Mr. Brighton would be almost sure to want to move back out to his farm if he had a family to help him take care of it.

The more he thought about it, the more Harry liked the Plan. There were a few problems, though. The main one was that the idea didn't seem to have occurred to Mom or Mr. Brighton. Having been around grownups so much, Harry thought he knew the symptoms. Like the time Miss Dutton, who lived in the east room for about a year, had married Mr. Jenkins, who stayed at Marco's once a month, when he was in the city selling stuff to beauty shops. After they got married Mr. Jenkins didn't come any more, because Miss Dutton made him stop traveling.

Anyway, it always started out the same, with lots of silly compliments and staring at each other. Then came whispering and holding hands and giving presents. As far as he could tell, Mom and Mr. Brighton didn't have a single symptom.

Mr. Brighton always seemed friendly enough where Mom was concerned. Sometimes he even offered to help her out with heavy jobs around the house. But Harry wasn't sure you could count that. It wasn't a sure sign at least, like whispering or holding hands.

That night in his room, Harry got as far as deciding that he was going to have to do something himself. That is, he was going to have to find a way to get Mom and Mr. Brighton to really notice each other. That part of the Plan was easy to see. The hard part was figuring out how he was going to do it. He finally went to sleep thinking that maybe Lee Furdell would have some ideas.

The next morning, right after his regular chores were done, Harry went next door to the candy store, looking for Lee. But this morning, Mrs. Furdell was behind the counter so Harry didn't go in. People were always looking for Lee Furdell. Everyone in the neighborhood who needed advice or sympathy, or even just a free taste of candy, went looking for him. Nobody ever looked for Olive Furdell, and if you found her by mistake you knew better than to ask her for anything; even a little piece of information, like where her husband was that morning. You just went on looking.

The candy store filled the entire front yard of the Furdell place, right up to the sidewalk, but a tiny narrow alley led around the side of the gingerbready old house to the back yard. Lee was in the back yard hanging out the wash. When he saw Harry, he stopped right away and sat down on the back steps to have a talk. Lee was like that.

"Well, sit down Harry," he said, patting a place beside him on the stair. "Let's catch up on the boarding house gossip. You haven't been to see me for so long. I'm afraid I'm all out of date."

Mr. Furdell was a small man with limp hair and big soft eyes, like some sort of woods animal. He didn't look very interesting until you got to know him. But everyone who knew him agreed that he was one of the greatest guys in the neighborhood. That is, everyone except his wife, maybe.

Ever since Harry first came to Kerry Street, he had been taking his broken toys, his kites that wouldn't fly, and his problems to Lee—that was what everybody called him, even kids. And Lee always had time to help —that is, unless his wife was around. Olive Furdell never seemed to like the way Lee spent so much time helping other people.

Lee hadn't heard about Miss Thurgood's leaving yet, so Harry started off by telling him about that. Lee smiled about Miss Thurgood sitting in the water—he wasn't the kind to laugh right out loud very much—and he said he would keep his ears open when he went to the candy store supply place that afternoon and see if he could hear of anyone who was looking for a good place to board.

Then Harry led into his main reason for coming. You'd think it would be hard to explain something as personal as trying to get your mother to marry somebody, but it really wasn't. You could tell Lee almost anything without feeling embarrassed.

"That's a funny thing," Lee said, when he finished.

"The very same possibility occurred to me some time ago. I liked Hal Brighton the first time I met him, and not long ago I was thinking that it would be a fine thing if he and Lorna Marco took a notion to get married. Running that big bording house *is* too hard a job for a woman all by herself, just as you say. And I'm inclined to think that you've picked a fine husband and father prospect. But you say you haven't noticed any symptoms that they're thinking along the same lines?"

"No," Harry said, "they like each other all right, you can tell that. But just friendly, you know."

Mr. Furdell sighed. "It's quite a problem," he said. "As a rule, it's a bit hard for a third party to influence these things, one way or the other. But there must be something you can do. I'm going to give it some careful thought."

Just then Olive Furdell called from inside the house, "Leland! Leland!" Her voice always went up high and screechy on the second syllable. Lee went back to the clothesline, and Harry headed for the alley.

"I'll think about it," Lee called over his shoulder, his voice coming out mumbly around the clothespin in his mouth. "I'll let you know if I think of anything."

Harry was halfway down the alley when Mrs. Furdell came out onto the back porch, but he heard every word she said. You had to be farther away than that to get out of earshot of Olive Furdell. "Leland, I swear to goodness, you're the slowest man alive. Are you going to take all day to hang up that little dab of wash?"

As far as Harry could tell, Lee didn't say anything at all. Harry took a hard kick at a little pebble on the sidewalk, sighed, and went on down the alley.

He didn't get another chance to talk to Lee that day. And even though he did a lot of thinking about it, he didn't come up with any good ideas for the Plan. That night, when he was helping Mom in the kitchen, he decided to bring up the subject of Mr. Brighton to see if he could find out just what Mom really thought about him. But he'd just gotten the conversation going, when the door bell rang.

When Harry opened the front door, there on the dimly lit veranda, stood Mr. Tarzack Mazzeeck. He was looking every bit as round and wrinkled and unreal as he had the day before. "Dear me," he said, "I do hope you still have a vacancy. One that I could have for three or four days."

Mr. Mazzeeck

Harry was really surprised when he opened the front door and found Mr. Mazzeeck standing there. He'd almost forgotten about him. Of course he had intended to tell Mom all about the suitcase and jumping off the bus and everything, but with all the excitement about Miss Thurgood, he'd just never gotten around to it. Actually he had remembered for a minute when Mom was being so worried over the money; but he'd decided it wasn't worth mentioning. For one thing, Mr. Mazzeeck had said he was a traveling salesman, so there wasn't any chance he'd be a permanent guest. And besides there had been a pretty good chance that he wouldn't show up at all.

But now, here he was on the doorstep, with the same great big suitcase and another smaller one. "Sure, Mr. Mazzeeck," Harry said, "we have a swell room for you. Come on in and sit down and I'll tell my mom you're here."

When Harry and Mom came back from the kitchen, Mr. Mazzeeck was perched on the edge of a chair hugging his big suitcase on his lap, just as he'd done on the bus bench. The little suitcase was on the floor by his feet. Harry introduced him to Mom, and Mom told him all the things he had to know about hours for meals, and being called in the morning. Then she got out the register for him to sign. He still had the suitcase on his lap and he tried to balance the registry on top of the suitcase to write his name. But he couldn't quite reach, and the whole thing kept wobbling around till the book got away from him and fell on the floor. So he finally put the suitcase down, but very carefully and right in front of his feet. Judging by his own past experience, Harry was pretty sure that it wasn't a very good place for it. Mr. Mazzeeck finished signing the book, stood up and, sure enough, he fell right over the suitcase. He probably would have gone smack on his face if Harry hadn't grabbed his arm. After he got his balance again he thanked Harry all over the place, but a second later, when Harry tried to pick up the suitcase to carry it upstairs for him, he jerked it away.

"No, no," he said. "I will carry that one. You may bring the other, if you please." And he started off up the stairs.

Harry looked back over his shoulder at Mom and grinned, and she grinned back and raised an eyebrow. Harry knew that she meant, "That's a strange one."

Mr. Mazzeeck was strange all right, you had to admit that. Strange and funny and sort of mysterious, too. But Harry couldn't help liking him. There was something about him that made Harry feel good. For one thing, it was easy to see that they had some things in common—like a handful of thumbs and two left feet.

In the next couple of days Harry didn't see much of Mr. Mazzeeck. Not that Harry was too busy with other things, or anything like that. As a matter of fact, he was around most of the time. He read a little, talked over the back fence to Lee once or twice, and worked some on his Plan, when he could think of something to do on it, anyway.

He did manage once to get Mom and Mr. Brighton out on the veranda together, one night after dinner. They didn't stay very long, but Harry was encouraged anyway. It was a typical summer night in San Francisco, and to stay outdoors at all without a coat, you'd have to be feeling pretty romantic.

Harry didn't see Mr. Mazzeeck just because he wasn't around the house very much. He went out in the morning with his big suitcase, and he didn't come back until almost dinner time. He didn't talk much at the table even when the other boarders asked him questions. He ate a lot, though, and Harry noticed he really did seem to enjoy the food—particularly Mom's good desserts.

It was because of noticing about the desserts that Harry happened to go into Mr. Mazzeeck's room. On the third night after his arrival at Marco's, Mr. Mazzeeck came back from wherever he went every day, too late for dinner. Mom and Harry were both in the living room when he came in, carrying his big suitcase and looking more tired and worried than ever.

"I was most distressed over missing one of your wonderful dinners, Mrs. Marco," he said, "but I was detained by a customer."

"Would you like to come out in the kitchen and let me warm something up for you?" Mom said. Mom must have thought that he looked pitiful, too, because she didn't usually do that sort of thing. If a boarder was late for dinner, it was just too bad for him. Mom had enough to do without cooking and washing dishes all over again.

"Oh, that is most kind of you, but no thank you. I wouldn't think of letting you go to so much trouble. Besides, I had a bite to eat at a restaurant."

But it seemed to Harry that he looked a bit wistful. It was that wistful look mostly, but also just plain curiosity, that sent Harry up to Mr. Mazzeeck's room a little later. You couldn't help wondering about such a strange little man with such a mysterious big suitcase. And there *had* been some pineapple upside-down cake left over from dinner.

So, at about eight o'clock, Harry knocked at the door of Mr. Mazzeeck's room with two pieces of cake and a cup of coffee on a tray. The door opened a little way, and Mr. Mazzeeck put his head out. He was wearing a sort of bathrobe thing with long flowing sleeves. It was dark purple with squiggly red figures all over it. When he saw the cake, his startled look changed to a smile—a hungry smile. He said, "My, my, doesn't that look delicious. How very thoughtful of you." He opened the door wide enough to let Harry in.

"Mom said I could have a bed-time snack," Harry said. "I thought you might like to keep me company. It's terrific cake."

"Quite so, quite so, I am delighted. Won't you sit

down." Mr. Mazzeeck got them both chairs, and when
they had started in on the cake he said, "You are, indeed, a most unusual young person. Let me see, you
said your name was Harry?"

"That's right, Harry Houdini Marco. My dad named me that. He was a magician, and he was crazy about Harry Houdini."

"Harry Houdini Marco? And the son of a magician. How remarkable. How extraordinarily remarkable." Mr. Mazzeeck stopped eating with a forkful of cake halfway to his mouth. Most people were interested or amused when Harry told them his full name, but Mr. Mazzeeck seemed absolutely flabbergasted. Harry was beginning to get a little uncomfortable when the man finally stopped staring and asked, "I suppose you have begun your training?"

"Training?"

"Yes, your apprenticeship. With whom are you studying the art of magic?"

"Oh, to be a magician, you mean. No, I'm not studying with anybody."

"Ah, that is a shame. You must begin soon now. The good ones all begin very young."

Harry had been getting ready to say that he just wasn't the magician type, but Mr. Mazzeeck sounded so enthusiastic that it seemed a shame to disappoint him. So he only said, "I guess you're right about that. My dad started practicing magic when he was just a little kid. He used to tell me about it. Are you a magician, too?"

"No, no," Mr. Mazzeeck said. "I am a salesman. I am only a traveling salesman, but at one time I was . . . I was something more than that." His voice trailed off into a sigh. For an uncomfortably long time he said nothing at all. Harry looked at him curiously, but Mr.

Mazzeeck didn't seem to notice. He looked different somehow, as he had that time before; his eyes were dark and hollow with remembering, as if they were looking backwards to a far, far past.

He began to say something, but not exactly to Harry. "So many years, so many changes . . ." he muttered. "Even magic changes . . . Most of it mere trickery now, mumbo-jumbo . . . Grand old dreams all forgotten . . . Nobody has the time and space any more . . ."

As Harry watched, wondering, he suddenly had a split-second impression, so strange and spooky that it made a shiver zig-zag up his spine. It was as if, for just a moment, Mr. Mazzeeck's funny chubby face had turned into a transparent mask, and from beneath it another face looked through. Another face, older and yet ageless, with eyes that burned with a deep dark power.

It was just a glimpse, and then Mr. Mazzeeck looked like himself again and his eyes seemed to come back into focus. "Take boys, for instance," he said, in an accusing tone of voice. "Do they dream of wielding Excalibur or taming Pegasus?" He shook his finger in Harry's face. "Or do your dreams rise no higher than a baseball bat or a bicycle?"

"Gee, Mr. Mazzeeck," Harry said. "I don't dream about things like that. I would like to have a new ten-speed, but I don't *dream* about it." He had been feeling pretty uneasy, and now he felt a little guilty, too, without really knowing why.

But just then Mr. Mazzeeck calmed down to his usual sort of nervous embarrassment. "I'm so sorry," he said. "I'm afraid I've been taking out my problems on you, and of course, you are entirely blameless. You must forgive me, but my business has not been going well lately, and I am very tired."

He stood up suddenly and put his empty plate back on the tray. "The cake was most delicious, and I find myself even more deeply indebted to you. You must visit me again, sometime."

Harry knew an invitation to leave when he heard one, but when he turned to pick up the tray, he noticed something that stopped him in his tracks. On the foot of the bed, with its top wide open, sat the mysterious suitcase. He took a step or two backwards; but almost as quickly, Mr. Mazzeeck must have realized what he was trying to do. He had time for only a tiny glimpse of the contents of the suitcase before Mr. Mazzeeck had stepped in front of it, hiding it from view.

Afterwards, Harry didn't quite remember what he'd said next or just how he'd said good-by. He had a general impression that they'd both been very polite and that Mr. Mazzeeck had asked him to come again. But it wasn't surprising that Harry's mind had been on something else, at the time. In fact, his mind was on that something else for a long, long time. It wasn't the kind of thing you could just forget about. You don't just forget that there is a strange man living in your own house who carries in his suitcase a long, sharp, evil-looking sword.

The Sword
and Other Problems

That night, Harry lay awake for hours, wondering and worrying. He didn't want to tell Mom and get her all worried, too, unless there really was a reason. And maybe there wasn't any reason. Maybe there was a perfectly understandable explanation of why a strange-acting little man should be sneaky and suspicious about his suitcase and why it should contain, among other strange-looking objects, a long, sharp, gleaming sword. The trouble was, it was pretty hard for Harry to imagine what that explanation could be.

He might be a professional sword swallower, for instance, except that wouldn't explain why he pretended to be a salesman, and why he was so secretive. There's no reason to pretend you're not a sword swallower if you are one.

Still, in spite of its weaknesses, that was just about the best possibility that Harry could come up with. Possibility! There was that word again! It was beginning to look as if the Swami were right and the air really was full of possibilities. Only right now, some of them were almost too awful to think about. Like, for instance, the fact that a boarding house might be a good place to hide in if you'd committed some terrible deed; the kind of deed you might do with a big—sword.

The worst of it was that if something terrible did happen, it would be Harry's fault. After all, he was the one who had asked Mr. Mazzeeck to come to the boarding house.

After lying awake half the night, Harry finally decided the best thing to do would be to keep quiet, for the time being, and just try to keep an eye on Mr. Mazzeeck. It wouldn't be for long. Mr. Mazzeeck had already been at Marco's for three days and he'd said something about three or four days when he arrived. Besides, it was very unusual for a traveling salesman to stay more than a few days at a time. But, of course, that sort of depended on whether Mr. Mazzeeck really was a traveling salesman.

It wasn't four days, or five, or even six. Mr. Mazzeeck was right there at Marco's for a whole week after that night when Harry first saw the sword. And during that week all sorts of terrible things happened. Not that Mr. Mazzeeck murdered anyone in his sleep or did any of the other awful things Harry had imagined. What did happen, were things that had never even occurred to him.

In the first place, it was the very next day that Clarissa Clyde came to stay at Marco's Boarding House. When Mom called Harry into the living room to carry Miss Clyde's bright red imitation alligator luggage upstairs, he didn't realize that more trouble had arrived. In fact, he was feeling pretty happy that they had a new boarder, who might be permanent. It was somebody to take Miss Thurgood's place—and someone who might be a little more interesting, too.

For one thing, Miss Clyde was a night club singer. He'd overheard her telling Mom so. That was something new and different for Marco's. As far as Harry could remember, they'd never had any kind of singer before. And even if Miss Clyde was strange looking, at least she was a change from Miss Thurgood.

Miss Clyde was a big woman, not fat exactly, but a good bit wider than Mom, at least in places. She was probably as old as Mom, but it was a little hard to tell because her real face was all cluttered over with make-up. Her hair was a stiff yellow color, like a doll in a store window, and her red and white dress looked as if it wasn't quite big enough to fit her.

But the happiness about having a new boarder didn't last very long; at least not for Harry. Right away, he found out one awful thing: she called people Sweetie. Everybody—even boys. When Harry got to the top of the stairs with her luggage, she gave him a dime and said, "There you go, Sweetie. Thanks a million."

That was bad enough, but something worse started happening that night at dinner. It began almost the very moment Mom introduced Miss Clyde to the rest of the boarders. Right away Miss Clyde popped herself down next to Mr. Brighton, and even before the very first meal was over she was calling him "Sweetie" and "Hal" and flopping her long sticky-looking eyelashes up and down.

Harry was really disgusted. He saw what she was

doing right away. It was just like when Miss Dutton started in on the beauty shop man, only about a million times worse. It was all so obvious you couldn't help noticing, but Mom didn't seem to. At least, she didn't fight back at all, like flopping her eyelashes, too, and giggling, or any of the other things women do when they want somebody's attention. Harry did the best he could by trying to start a conversation with Mr. Brighton about the Giants' shut-out game against the Dodgers. But Mr. Brighton didn't seem to be in the mood for baseball. It was a terrible meal.

By that evening Harry had decided that there wasn't anything he could do about Clarissa Clyde, at least not right then; but it was that very night that he thought of something he could do about Mr. Mazzeeck. Or, at least, something that might help him find out what the guy was up to. The thing that occurred to him was that there was a way to look in the window of Mr. Mazzeeck's room.

The old carriage house on the Furdell place was right next to the edge of Marco's property. It was a huge old barn-like place with all sorts of curly wood-trimmings. It had a slanted roof and above that a little flat one, like a platform, with a railing around it. There were stairs that led up to the flat roof on the outside of the building. Mr. Furdell said that his grandfather used to be a ship's captain, and he had had it built that way so he could watch the ships on the bay.

Anyway, there was a swell view from up there, and if you looked towards the west you could look right into the second-story windows of the two old houses.

Harry waited until it was good and dark before he slipped through the gate to the Furdell's yard and up the stairs to the roof of the carriage house. Just as he had hoped, the blind was up in Mr. Mazzeeck's room and the light was on. Harry could clearly see the picture of a vase of roses and an apple on the opposite side of the room, but for a long time he didn't see anything of Mr. Mazzeeck. If he was in the room he certainly wasn't moving around much.

It seemed like more than an hour that Harry knelt behind the railing and peered into Mr. Mazzeeck's room. At least it was long enough for him to get awfully cold and damp and stiff. Then, just as he made up his mind to give up, he saw Mr. Mazzeeck walk across the room.

Harry sat back down with a thump. A few seconds later, Mr. Mazzeeck came back across the room looking at something in his hands. He crossed the room to the window and glanced out. Harry caught just a glimpse of the thing in his hands—something golden and shiny— before Mr. Mazzeeck pulled down the blind.

But at that point Mr. Mazzeeck made a mistake. He didn't seem to realize that even though the shade was down, the window could still be dangerous. It didn't seem to occur to him that if he really didn't want to be seen, he shouldn't stand so near a thin window-shade with a light on behind him.

Immediately there appeared on the window-shade a short, well-rounded silhouette, as clear and sharp as the figures in a magic lantern show. It was unmistakably Mr. Mazzeeck, and he appeared to be doing something with the object in his hands.

Harry felt a thrill of awful anticipation, like when the background music in a horror picture tells you that something terrible is about to leap out at you. It didn't exactly look like a sword in Mr. Mazzeeck's hands; but maybe that was only because of the angle the light was hitting it. ·

Then, as the imaginary horror music reached a brain-numbing climax, Harry realized that Mr. Mazzeck was not alone in his room. Harry was sure he hadn't so much as blinked, but somehow he had missed the arrival of the huge shadowy figure that now faced the shorter, rounder silhouette. The other man seemed to have a huge head and shoulders, and as he towered over Mr. Mazzeeck, he swayed backward and forward, as if he were unsteady on his feet.

For less than a minute, hardly long enough for Harry to convince himself that he was really seeing it, the second figure in Mr. Mazzeeck's room cast its shadow against the shade. Then, while Harry still stared in unblinking fascination, it began to change. First, it became softer and less distinct; it wavered more than ever and became blurry around the edges. Then suddenly, it shrank away to nothing. The shorter shadow stayed for a moment; then it disappeared too. But it only seemed to walk away from the window.

It was some time before Harry began to realize that he was in a very uncomfortable position on the roof of the carriage house. He was cold and stiff, and he had been staring at the golden rectangle of window-shade for so long that he felt a little cross-eyed. He had to blink several times and rub his eyes before he could focus well enough to find his way down the stairs and across the yard to the back door.

On his way upstairs he stopped for a moment and listened outside Mr. Mazzeeck's door, but everything was quiet. Up in his own room, he threw himself down on the bed and thought and thought and thought.

Who was the other man in Mr. Mazzeeck's room? What had Mr. Mazzeeck been holding in his hands? If someone fell to the floor in front of a window, would his shadow on the shade appear to shrink away?

The longer Harry thought about it, the harder it was to remember just exactly what he had seen. By the time he gave up trying to figure it out, he wasn't at all sure he hadn't imagined the whole thing.

The next few days were terrible, at least in the mornings and evenings when all the borders were home. It turned out that Miss Clyde really lived on what she called her "private income" and only had "occasional engagements" at night clubs. Mom said she thought Miss Clyde got alimony from somebody she used to be married to, but Harry had seen her once in the hall without her make-up, and he figured that maybe the "private income" was an old age pension. Anyway she didn't go to work much, so she was around the boarding house an awful lot.

Harry was just about going crazy, trying to keep his eye on Mr. Mazzeeck and Miss Clyde and Mr. Brighton all at the same time. And as if things weren't bad enough, he started having to keep a watch on Mom and Mr. Konkel, too.

Harry had always known that Mr. Konkel was sort of gone on Mom, but he'd never worried about it, because it was pretty plain that Mom didn't like him any more than Harry did. And that wasn't much. In fact, Harry and Mom had had a joke about Mr. Konkel for a long time. When no one else was around, of course, Mom would say something like, "There goes Oscar Konkel, the man-like machine."

"It walks, it talks, it breathes, it's almost human," Harry would say, "but it has a ticker tape for a heart."

"And a slide rule for a brain," Mom would add. Sometimes they got so funny on the subject, that for a day or two they couldn't look at each other when Mr. Konkel was around without wanting to giggle.

But now, all of a sudden, Mom changed. She started to listen to Mr. Konkel's long boring stories about how he solved the mystery of the missing decimal point, or how he caught a sneaky grocery clerk, red-handed, trying to rob him of two cents change. She let Mr. Konkel give her a box of candy, and one night she even went for a walk with him.

For once Lee wasn't being much help, either. He hadn't come up with any good ideas about Mom and Mr. Brighton, yet, and when Harry told him about Miss Clyde, all he said was that it might be a good thing if she would go some place else to board.

Harry already knew that, for Pete Squeaks! The problem was how to get her to go.

It seemed all in all as if things couldn't get much worse.

A Midnight Visitor

Mr. Mazzeeck stayed and stayed, and Harry got more and more nervous about him. On the evening of the eleventh day, Harry was feeling very tired and discouraged. Mr. Brighton had actually taken Miss Clyde out—that is, he was going somewhere and Miss Clyde had asked him for a lift downtown. So maybe they were together somewhere without Harry around to keep an eye on them.

All evening long Harry had been stuck in the living room with nothing at all to do. He hadn't been able to leave because he'd had to watch Mom and Mr. Konkel. Mr. Konkel was teaching Mom to play chess. Chess was the only game that Mr. Konkel enjoyed playing, because, according to him, you had to play by a formula; and if you were a good enough player, the whole thing was predictable from the very beginning.

Harry climbed into bed that night wishing he were too worried to be tired, or too tired to be worried; instead of a whole lot of both. It was some time after he had finally worried himself to sleep that he woke up suddenly and completely. He had a very strong feeling that he'd heard something. Not traffic noise or a foghorn on the bay, but a small sound very close to his bed. He waited for a moment, holding his breath, and the noise came again. Someone was knocking on his door.

Harry fought down an urge to pull the covers up over his head and just lie there. Instead, he swallowed hard, slipped out of bed, and opened the door just a crack. He peeked out and found himself nose to nose with Mr. Mazzeeck.

"Ah," Mr. Mazzeeck said. "There you are. I am so sorry to disturb your slumber, but I must see you tonight. It's most urgent."

Harry swallowed hard again and opened the door just a tiny bit wider. There was no sign of a sword. So after one or two more gulps he managed to say, "Sure, Mr. Mazzeeck. What can I do for you?"

"Come with me, please. We must go to my room." He turned and started down the narrow third-floor stairs, and Harry grabbed his robe and followed. By the pale flickering light he could make out that Mr. Mazzeeck was not wearing the purple bathrobe that he'd had on the day Harry had brought him the cake. He was all dressed up in his funny-looking suit and overcoat. It was just about then that Harry noticed what was making the flickering light. The hall lights were out and Mr. Mazzeeck was lighting his way with—not a flashlight—not even a candle, which would have been strange enough —but with a lamp. The lamp seemed to be made of brass or bronze. It was oval-shaped and had a little pedestal, by which Mr. Mazzeeck was carrying it. A small flickering flame burned at one end of the oval.

Harry was so amazed and fascinated that he forgot to look where he was going, and just as they reached the bottom of the stairs he cracked his toe on a baluster. It was a bad bump—just about as painful as a stubbed toe can possibly be. But there was one good thing about it—it made Harry so darned mad that he forgot to be frightened. He just hobbled right into Mr. Mazzeeck's room, sat down on the bed, and began rubbing his toe. Mr. Mazzeeck put the lamp on the bed table and sat down in a chair.

"Did you injure yourself?" he asked anxiously.

"Oh, no," Harry said. "It's just a stubbed toe. I'm used to them."

"I'm very sorry. I feel I am responsible."

"It's nothing," Harry said. "It doesn't hurt."

"Well then, I shall attempt to explain my nocturnal call. You must be very puzzled."

Harry shrugged and tried to look as if mysterious midnight visitors didn't bother him a bit.

"You see," Mr. Mazzeeck went on, "I had intended to arrange this interview at a more conventional hour; however, I have just received word from my superiors that I must proceed at once to my next assignment. As you see, I am leaving immediately." He gestured toward the closet door, and Harry noticed for the first time that it was open and the closet was quite empty. On a chair near the closet was the small suitcase. The little table had been pulled out into the middle of the room and the big suitcase was sitting on it. The lid was down, but Harry noticed that the three heavy, old-fashioned latches were not fastened.

"Firstly," Mr. Mazzeeck went on, "I want to tell you how very grateful I am to you. Not only for returning my suitcase to me when we first met, but also for my pleasant stay in your mother's home. I have not been so comfortable since . . . well, since I started upon my wanderings. And the food—ah—it was delicious." Mr. Mazzeeck's wrinkled cherub-face smoothed into a faraway look, as if he were in the midst of a pleasant dream. Harry waited until Mr. Mazzeeck reluctantly pulled his mind away from Mom's pies and cakes and went on with his story. "I'll have to admit," he said, "that I have purposely prolonged my stay because I hated to leave such comfortable surroundings."

Harry couldn't help smiling a bit. He'd suspected Mr. Mazzeeck of hanging around longer than necessary —but Harry imagined he was waiting for an opportunity to use that sword on someone. And all he'd really been after was a few more home-cooked meals. The thought made Harry feel so good that he got generous. "Well, we've enjoyed having you as a guest," he said. "We'll be looking forward to having you stop here the next time you're in San Francisco."

Mr. Mazzeeck suddenly looked very sad. "Ah," he said, "I'd like that, but I'm afraid it's impossible. You see, the next time I return to San Francisco, you and your lovely mother will no longer be alive."

For a minute, Harry didn't believe his ears, and then it felt like his heart exploded in an enormous shattering thump. So Mr. Mazzeeck *was* a crazy man, after all—and he did have plans for that terrible sword. Harry got up stiffy, and started backing toward the door.

A Strange Gift

As Harry backed away toward the door, his face must have shown the horror he felt, because Mr. Mazzeeck suddenly seemed to realize what he had just said. He struck himself impatiently on the forehead. "Wait a moment. How foolish of me. You don't understand, of course. You must let me explain."

Harry stopped backing up, but he didn't come any closer.

"You must understand," Mr. Mazzeeck went on, "that you shall not be alive when I return to San Francisco, only because my orders do not include another trip to this area until the year 2071."

"The year 2071?" Harry gasped. "You must be kidding."

"No, it is quite true."

"How—er—how old will *you* be then—in 2071?" Harry asked edging back a bit into the room. He was beginning to be pretty sure that Mr. Mazzeeck wasn't dangerous. Crazy maybe, but not dangerous.

Mr. Mazzeeck thought a moment. "Just a bit over 3,000 years," he said. He smiled his sad little smile.

"You must have guessed by now that I'm not an ordinary peddler."

"Well, I did notice that you were—uh—not too ordinary," Harry admitted.

"Yes," Mr. Mazzeeck said. "You see, I am an employee of the A. A. Comus Company and, although I am no longer a sorcerer myself, I am still a member of the A.O.A.T.S., with some of its rights and privileges; among which is, of course, immortality." He looked at Harry significantly, as if Harry should know what he was talking about.

"The A.O.A. . . . what?" Harry said.

"The A.O.A.T.S. The Ancient Order of Authentic and Traditional Sorcerers. I was once a full member." Mr. Mazzeeck drew himself up to his full height, raised his chin and for just a moment Harry thought he saw again that strange transparency that seemed to let another face look through. A face lit, this time, by a deep, glowing pride. Then Mr. Mazzeeck was himself again, only a little sadder and more worried looking. "I am now only a Peddler and Purveyor of the Finest and Most Traditional of Magical Goods."

"Oh," Harry said, "you mean you sell magic stuff to magicians and things like that?"

"No indeed. Not if you mean boxes with false backs and other gimcracks of that nature to ordinary commercial magicians. I do have some dealings with magicians, however, but only the most gifted and most dedicated, and then only after careful investigation. Your father was under consideration at the time of his death, my superiors tell me. They felt he had great talent and showed real promise. It was that fact, plus my immense gratitude, that made it possible for me to receive permission from the company to present you with a small sample of its products."

All the fancy language had left Harry a little bit behind, but he thought it meant that Mr. Mazzeeck intended to give him something—something out of the mysterious suitcase, perhaps. "Well, gee—thanks!" he said, just in case he was right.

"Don't mention it," Mr. Mazzeeck said. "I feel it's the least I can do. With your background, not to mention what I have observed of your skillfulness and reliability, I'm sure I will have no cause to regret my decision."

"Skillfulness? Me?" Harry asked incredulously, but Mr. Mazzeeck had gone over to the suitcase and opened the lid.

"Our only problem now," Mr. Mazzeeck said, rummaging around among the contents, "is to decide what would be more appropriate. There are many possibilities and we must make the decision with the utmost care. That is one of the major tenets of the Comus Company. All our clients must not only be deserving, but their purchases must also be carefully chosen."

He picked out something and held it up for Harry to see. It was a ring that seemed to be made of the bodies of two little golden snakes twisted tightly around each other. He looked at it thoughtfully for a moment and then shook his head and replaced it in the case. "No," he said, "I don't think so." He smiled apologetically at Harry. "You can't imagine the predicaments one can get oneself into by the careless use of three wishes, if one is inexperienced in such matters. Have you ever had three wishes?"

"Well, no," Harry said. "I don't think I've had even one."

"Ah, you see. Then we can rule out wishing rings and stones at the same time, I'm afraid, we must eliminate the various containers of genii. They are a bit more versatile than the rings, but in the hands of a beginner, the results are often much the same."

Harry had been edging forward until now he was standing beside the table. "You mean you have real magic genii in there?"

"Yes indeed. We have them, not only in bottles," Mr. Mazzeeck held up a small bottle of dark glass that seemed to be full of a whirling white smoke, "but also in the more traditional bronze lamp." At that point he began to paw around in the suitcase with a frantic look on his face. "The lamp," he muttered as if he were talking to himself. "Where is the lamp. It's not possible I could have lost it."

"Is that what you're looking for?" Harry said, pointing to the oval-shaped thing that was still burning on the bed table.

"Ah! Of course," Mr. Mazzeeck said looking terribly relieved. "I had forgotten that I used it to light my way to your room."

By now Harry was in a position to see into the suitcase. He pointed to something that looked only too familiar. "What's that?" he asked. The long golden sword was one of the largest things in the case.

Mr. Mazzeeck took it out and ran his hand lovingly over the gleaming blade. Harry couldn't help taking a step or two backwards. "Beautiful, isn't it?" Mr. Mazzeeck said. "Notice the careful setting of the gems in the hilt, and the intricate design. However, I'm afraid that this is not quite the gift for you either. Actually there is very little use for these in this day and age. I carry this one with me mostly for old time's sake. One so seldom hears of dragons to be slain or multi-headed beasts to be vanquished, any more. It's a great pity, but the demand for magic swords has almost disappeared."

Mr. Mazzeeck put the sword back in the case and took out something that looked like a black cape of a silky material. "I don't suppose you've ever had any particular desire to be invisible?" he asked.

"Well, no, but . . ."

"No, I didn't suppose you would have. Truthfully, I can't see how it would be of any great use to you. And with a mother who cooks as well as yours does, I can't see that you are greatly in need of a magic porridge pot, or tablecloth either. Dear me, this is proving to be more of a problem than I had anticipated."

Next, Mr. Mazzeeck took what appeared to be a rolled-up throw-rug out of the case with one hand and a strange-looking pair of high-topped boots with the other. "How about travel?" he asked. "I could let you have either a magic carpet or seven league boots."

"Travel?" Harry said. He still didn't believe that Mr. Mazzeeck was serious, but you couldn't help sort of getting into the spirit of the thing. "Well, I'm not too crazy about traveling, but I would like to be somewhere else for a while. Can you take anyone with you?"

"No, I'm afraid not. And I see now, that there would be difficulties. You couldn't very well go off and leave your mother. It's quite obvious she depends on you."

"What's that?" Harry asked, pointing to something long and thin and silvery.

Mr. Mazzeeck gave a little shudder. "That," he said, "is a flute. Frankly, it's not one of my favorite items. Not that it doesn't do the job it's supposed to do," he added hastily. "It's just that . . . well it was this particular item that figured in my disgrace and demotion." He picked up the long shiny flute and turned it over and over so that it sparkled in the light. "A pretty thing, isn't it," he said. "One would never guess by looking at it that it could be the cause of so much grief."

"What happened?" Harry asked. "That is, if you don't mind talking about it."

"No," Mr. Mazzeeck said. "I don't mind. As a matter of fact, it's a relief to discuss it now and then. Get it off my chest, you might say. It's not often that I meet someone to whom I can talk about matters of this sort. But since you have been cleared by the company . . ." Suddenly Mr. Mazzeeck looked at his watch and then hastily glanced at the bed and motioned for Harry to sit down. "My taxi won't be here for several minutes," he said. "Would you care to hear the whole story? I'm not keeping you from anything?"

Harry shook his head quickly and sat down. He was every bit as eager to hear Mr. Mazzeeck's story as Mr. Mazzeeck seemed to be to tell it.

Mr. Mazzeeck continued to stand by the case, fingering the lid with one hand and sometimes opening it. "As I mentioned earlier," he began, "I was once a sorcerer. And in all modesty I must say that I was an unusually successful one. I had a very choice assignment in which I was able to practice a bit of magic myself besides supplying a most distinguished clientele—the most renowned heroes of the day—all legendary now. But in my confidence, I overstepped myself and became involved in a duel with an unscrupulous wizard. This wizard—who called himself Mog—took pleasure in playing unseemly tricks on whatever victims he could entice. As an official of the Comus Company, I should have had nothing whatever to do with such a personage. But I allowed myself to become annoyed at Mog's interference in the affairs of one of my clients, and before I knew how it had happened, I was embroiled in a contest of magical strength. The contest itself would make a long story, spells and counter-spells, conjurations, invocations and incantations. Of course, I was duty bound to avoid anything but the most honorable in the world of magic. Alas, my opponent was not so bound, and in the end, by sheer trickery, I found myself caught in an evil enchantment."

"You mean you're enchanted right now?" Harry asked.

Slowly and sorrowfully Mr. Mazzeeck nodded his head.

Harry's mind raced over what he'd read about being enchanted, and suddenly he remembered the strange feeling he'd had once or twice that Mr. Mazzeeck was

somehow in disguise. "You mean you used to be somebody else, and this Mog turned you into—uh—the way you are now?"

"Not exactly. You are correct in guessing that the rather undignified and inconsequential form you see before you is not my true appearance. But that is not a part of the enchantment. No, my present shape is only the company's idea of what a traveling salesman should look like. Properly ordinary and unimpressive, but—" he glanced down at himself and shook his head uncertainly, "perhaps a bit out of date, at this point. Don't you think?"

Harry ignored the question. He was most interested in the idea of being enchanted. "But what is the enchantment, then?" he asked.

"Oh, it's nothing tragic or dramatic," Mr. Mazzeeck said. "That wouldn't have been Mog's style. The whole thing was so despicably handled that I didn't even realize I'd been enchanted until after I began to make mistakes. Sorcerers are not given to error, so after several serious blunders, I investigated. Of course I soon turned up the reason, but it was far too late to fend off the curse then. As I recall, the incantation went something like this:

> *He whom Mog has cause to hate*
> *Is doomed to botch and blunder.*
> *A dunderhead, an addlepate,*
> *He'll bungle and miscalculate*
> *He'll slip and miss—until the date*
> *This spell is burst asunder."*

Mr. Mazzeeck shuddered with remembered horror. "It was a terrible shock," he said. "Mog was captured and finally destroyed by the company, but nothing would destroy the spell. I continued to make mistakes and errors until at last the company was forced to demote me. I was stripped of my rank and forbidden the use of any kind of magic. Actually I was fortunate to be kept on as a simple salesman. The company was not to blame, you understand. One cannot allow incompetence when one deals with a powerful and dangerous product."

"But what happened about the flute?" Harry asked.

"Ah, yes, the flute. That was the last straw. After the flute incident there was nothing my superiors could do but demote me. You see, I was filling an order for a magic flute for a fellow who said he intended to use it to exterminate rats in a little town in Germany. But I must have made a mistake in the formula, and the flute was given too wide a range. It was used not only on rats but also to commit a deed so horrible that it has become a legend. The public outcry was tremendous; and, of course, the scandal touched the Comus Company. And that is just the sort of thing they have always taken every precaution to avoid."

There was something vaguely familiar about the flute story, but Harry was too busy thinking about the enchantment to figure it out. "Did the enchantment keep on working? I mean, even now when you aren't a sorcerer any more?"

"Oh dear, yes. I'm afraid so. It's just that my mistakes are of smaller consequence now. I loose train tickets and," he smiled ruefully, "fall out of buses."

Harry couldn't help feeling sympathetic. "Isn't there any chance that you'll get over it? The enchantment, I mean."

"There is one faint hope," Mr. Mazzeeck said. "According to one old and obscure book on spells, there *is* a way to escape." Mr. Mazzeeck reached into a pocket inside his coat and brought out a worn and discolored scrap of paper. He unfolded it carefully and handed it to Harry. The fancy faded print said:

> *Mog will not remove a curse,*
> *Till Better triumphs over Worst.*
> *Till Bad-to-Worse*
> *Has been Reversed*
> *And out of Error—Good has Burst.*

"Unfortunately, it's not the kind of thing that's likely to happen." Mr. Mazzeeck said, taking the paper from Harry and putting it away. "But I always carry it with me to keep up my spirits. Even a faint hope is better than none."

Harry hadn't understood much of what he had read, but he was inclined to agree that it didn't sound too likely.

"And in the meantime," Mr. Mazzeeck went on, "I am a wanderer. All over the world . . . places where magic is unappreciated or practically unknown . . . hard beds . . . tired feet . . . terrible food . . . here one day and gone the next . . . trains, ships, buses, and taxis."

"Why don't you fly?" Harry asked. "Wouldn't it be faster?"

Mr. Mazzeeck looked a little embarrassed. "I'm afraid I'm a bit old-fashioned, but aeroplanes make me uneasy. Don't they make you a bit nervous?"

"Well, no," Harry said. "I haven't flown any lately, but I used to a lot when I was a little kid and I loved it. But that's not exactly what I meant. I meant this way." He pointed to the rolled-up carpet in the suitcase.

"Ah, but don't you see, that is not possible. When I was deprived of my sorcerer's credentials, I was expressly forbidden the use of the company's products. It has been a hard sentence. I often yearn for the days when I could make use of the magic that I am now forbidden." Mr. Mazzeeck's eyes went dreamy. "Particularly the magic tablecloth," he murmured.

"You mean you can't use any of these things yourself?" Harry asked.

"Almost none. I am allowed a limited use of the lamp."

"You mean, like when you used it to come up to my room?"

"No," Mr. Mazzeeck said. "That's not the use I was referring to. I am allowed to summon the genii of this particular lamp, but only as a means of communication with my superiors at the head office. In fact, my orders to leave San Francisco tonight were brought by genii. It's a bit faster than airmail."

"I guess it would be, at that." Harry said.

Mr. Mazzeeck reached into his pocket and took out his big old watch. "Dear me," he said. "I must be going if I am to catch my train. We must make our decision quickly." He opened the lid all the way and stood staring

79

into the suitcase. Then his face crinkled into a smile. "Of course. What could be better?" He dug hastily through the jumble and came up with a small object that seemed to be a tiny silver vase or bottle. The metal looked thick and heavy, and it was engraved all over with a pattern of what appeared to be tiny leaves or feathers.

"There you are," Mr. Mazzeeck said, handing it to Harry. "A small token of my everlasting gratitude."

"Er—thanks. Thanks a lot," Harry said.

"Go on, open it."

The deeply embossed silver top was attached to a wide wooden cork. Inside the bottle there was a thick white liquid that looked very much like the stuff ladies put on their hands when they finish doing the dishes. "What is it?" Harry asked.

"Well, in our new catalogue it's listed as Volo Oil," Mr. Mazzeeck said disapprovingly. "But actually it's a very old product. Not one of these gadgety bits of trickery that are so popular nowadays, you can be sure of that. The ointment is made from a formula that has been known to the better sorcerers for centuries. The raw material is distilled from one of the oldest dreams of mankind. And it's only necessary to use one drop on each shoulder, rubbed in well. And of course, one must read the incantation on the label. Oh yes, and don't forget that the verse at the bottom of the label is necessary in order to return the user to his former state."

Harry turned the bottle around and noticed a smooth oval-shaped area where there was no engraving except for a few lines of very tiny print. He was trying to make out the words, when a horn honked right in front of the boarding house.

"That must be my taxi," Mr. Mazzeeck said. "I must be off. And I now have yet another reason to thank you. It was kind of you to listen so sympathetically to an old man's troubles. If I may presume on your kindness just once more to help me to the street with my luggage, I'll be on my way."

Harry had a million questions ready to ask, but Mr. Mazzeeck had already closed and fastened both his suitcases and started for the door with the large one. Harry could only stuff his gift into his pocket, pick up the other bag, and follow. In the rush down the stairs and into the taxi, there wasn't a chance for even one question, but after the driver had gotten back into his seat, Mr. Mazzeeck leaned out the window.

He spoke softly, behind his hand. "Once again, good-by, and thank you," he said. "And Harry, just a word or two of warning. As with all good magic, there is a bit of skill involved, so proceed with caution, particularly right at first. And above all use discretion. Remember, there must be absolutely no *public notice!* If a breath of this should get into the papers, your gift will be reclaimed, and I will be in trouble again. In my position that can only mean transfer to a subsidiary branch. I might even be assigned to the Voo Doo Line. You may not understand just what that would mean, but try to imagine how it would be for a man who has supplied the greatest heroes of myth and legend, to be forced to end his career peddling crocodiles' tongues and bats' gizzards to second-rate witches."

"Gee, Mr. Mazzeeck," Harry whispered, "I wouldn't

want to get you into any trouble. If you think I might, maybe I better not keep the—uh—what you gave me."

"Not at all," Mr. Mazzeeck said. "If you are careful, there should be no problem. The company cleared you for a gift, you know; I was only responsible for picking the right one." Then he smiled archly, the way people do when they're going to pay you a compliment. "I had no difficulty in getting the authorization. There's even a prophecy in your favor."

"A prophecy!" Harry gasped. "How did . . ."

But at that moment the taxi driver started the motor. Mr. Mazzeeck leaned out and took Harry's wrist in a firm clasp. "You must promise me that you'll be careful."

"Sure, Mr. Mazzeeck. I'll be careful as anything." Harry had the funny feeling that he hadn't the slightest notion what he was promising, but you just couldn't refuse anyone who looked so desperate.

All the tiny crinkles in Mr. Mazzeeck's face rearranged themselves into a few deep smile-lines. "I'm sure you will," he said. Then he leaned forward and spoke to the driver. "The train station, if you please." The taxi pulled away down Kerry Street, turned the corner, and disappeared from view.

The Last Possibility

Like someone in a dream, Harry walked back into the house and up the stairs. On the first landing he ran into Mom. "What's going on?" she asked. "I keep hearing people going up and down the stairs."

"Mr. Mazzeeck just left," Harry said. "I helped him carry his luggage out to the taxi."

"That's strange. He didn't say anything about leaving tonight at dinner. And he's all paid up until Thursday."

"He said he'd just heard from his boss, or something," Harry said. "I guess it was sort of unexpected."

Mom went back into her room shaking her head in a puzzled way, and Harry went on up the stairs to the third floor. Not until he had settled himself in his favorite spot on the foot of his bed, did he reach into his pocket. Now that he was back in his own room, with the familiar fog drifting past the window, he felt quite sure there would be nothing there at all. His pocket would be empty.

But it was there, all right. A small bottle of heavy silver, the deeply embossed pattern sharp and clear against his fingers. He just sat there, running his fingers over the rough surface and thinking.

There were two or three possibilities, and they were all so fascinating that Harry just barely noticed that he was fooling around with the old Swami's favorite word again. Anyway, the most likely one was that Mr. Mazzeeck was a little crazy, in an interesting sort of way. Or else, it could be that he was one of those people who go in for elaborate and carefully worked out jokes.

The last possibility was—well, if there was any other possibility it would have to be that Mr. Mazzeeck was neither joking nor crazy, and the little silver bottle in his pocket was full of some kind of magic—for Pete Squeaks!

It seemed pretty dumb to believe a thing like that, and yet, sitting there in the dark, with the summer fog wisping past his window, Harry found himself admitting that he'd known all along Mr. Mazzeeck was a lot more than he seemed on the surface. And that one admission, like a hole in the dike, let in a whole flood of new possibilities. For instance, there was the possibility that the towering, wavering figure Harry had seen through Mr. Mazzeeck's window had been a—well, a genie messenger, maybe. And it was even possible that Mr. Mazzeeck's shadowy face-behind-a-face hadn't been just Harry's imagination after all. Time went by, and as Harry sat holding the little bottle, the ordinary world of Marco's Boarding House, Kerry Street, San Francisco, U.S.A., began to grow dim and distant behind a glowing, flowing world of possibilities, too fantastic to put into words.

Suddenly Harry scooted over and turned on his bed

lamp, jerked the bottle out of his pocket, and pulled out the cork. The thick white liquid still looked a lot like hand lotion, but as he stared at it he began to see things he hadn't noticed before. For one thing, it glowed. A soft pearly light shone upwards from somewhere deep inside the bottle; and tiny ripples coiled and uncoiled no matter how still the bottle was held. Suddenly, like an echoing ripple, a deep shiver wound its way slowly from one end of Harry to the other. It was magic, all right, he was sure of it. Magic, magic, magic!

With the shiver still tingling in his finger tips, Harry started trying to recall everything Mr. Mazzeeck had told him about the silver bottle. Let's see—a drop on each shoulder, rubbed in well. And you were to recite the words that were written on the label. Harry held the bottle close to the light. It wasn't easy to read, and it didn't make much sense when you got it read, but it seemed to say:

> *Wing feather, bat leather, hollow bone,*
> *Gift of Icarus and Oberon,*
> *Dream of the earthbound—Spin and Flow*
> *Fledge and Flutter and Fan and GO!*

Then there was a line, and in the bottom half of the oval, it said:

> *Dream of the earthbound—Spin and Flow*
> *Flicker and Furl and Fold and NO!*

Harry read it over thoughtfully two or three times.

He didn't remember Mr. Mazzeeck's exact words, but he'd indicated that the short verse below the line was to make the, whatever it was, go away, when you were through with it. That was a good thing to remember. In stories and things there were always people who got into trouble because they forgot that part of the magic. With this thought in mind, Harry took time to say both verses over until he was sure he had them memorized.

At last, when he was positive it was all firmly in his head, he took off his robe and the tops of his pajamas. His hand was only a little shaky as he held the bottle over his bare shoulder. But he didn't tip it right away. Instead he started thinking again.

Some of the possibilities that had occurred to him had seemed great when he thought of them a moment or two ago. But now when they were staring him right in the face, they were almost too exciting. What if the stuff in the bottle turned him into something else? Maybe he wasn't always too crazy about being Harry Marco, but when it came right down to it, there were a lot of worse things a guy could be. In stories, people sometimes got changed into something really gruesome, like a big fat slimy toad. Or else they shrank away to almost nothing, or grew into a giant. Or—maybe the magic in the bottle might make you just disappear and turn up somewhere else, in some other century, even. Or what if . . .

All of a sudden Harry shook his head hard, took a firm grip on his imagination, and clenching his teeth he tipped the bottle—just a tiny bit.

The drops came out like tear-shaped pearls, and they seemed to fall very slowly. On the skin of his bare shoulders, they were neither cold nor hot, but tingling, as the touch of a sounding tuning fork. He crossed his arms and rubbed both shoulders, and the tingle grew and spread; all across his back and down deeper and deeper, until it seemed to come from some place inside him that he had never known about. He waited, but that was all—only the deep tingling and a maddening almost-but-not-quite feeling, like when something teeters on the very edge of—of what? Harry took a deep breath, shut his eyes, and very slowly and deliberately recited the incantation:

Wing feather, bat leather, hollow bone,
Gift of Icarus and Oberon,
Dream of the earthbound—Spin and Flow
Fledge and Flutter and Fan and GO!

As Harry said the last word he was instantly shaken by a violent and frightening sensation. There was no pain, but something seemed to press and pull and wrench deep inside his back. He couldn't seem to open his eyes, and a whirling dizziness made him stagger forward.

For a time—a strange amount of time that seemed to have very little to do with ordinary minutes or hours—the dark dizzy cloud whirled in his head and then, suddenly, it spun itself clear and drifted away. Harry found himself holding on to the bedpost with both hands. The violence was completely gone and he felt quite normal again, except for a heaviness across his shoulders as if a pack was strapped to them. He looked behind him—and almost yelled out loud.

Arching up behind him, higher than the top of his head was a huge—he looked the other way and there was another one—running to the mirror over his dresser, he turned sideways and there they were! Wings! Two great enormous wings sprang up from his shoulders, arched behind his head and swept down to his ankles in a long smooth line.

Harry's first gasp of surprise turned into a great ballooning rush of happiness. It was an absolutely fantastic feeling, as if his oldest dream or most impossible wish had just come true. Actually, he couldn't remember ever having wished for wings, at least, not in so many words. Not in the way that he'd wished that Mom didn't have to work so hard, that they could move to a ranch, or that he could get over being so clumsy. But now, all of a sudden, it was quite clear that wings were something he'd always wanted. Having wings was a dream that he seemed to know all about—not with his mind, but in a way that was older and more important than just remembering.

Along with that first rush of happiness came a strange kind of pride. Not nose-in-the-air human pride, but a joyous sort of proudness—like a peacock rejoicing over his beautiful tail. The wings were terrific to look at, covered closely and smoothly with soft shiny feathers, not white exactly, but more like the color of a cloud when the moon is behind it. Near the arched tops, the feathers were very small and curved to fit the line of bone and muscle. But farther down they got larger and larger until, at the tips, they looked bigger and stronger than any feathers Harry had ever seen.

Turning backward and forward, Harry looked and looked and looked. Then he reached back and touched one of the wings with his fingers. It felt warm and alive, and to his surprise he realized that the wing could feel. That is, not only were his fingers feeling the soft feathers over firm muscle, but his wings were feeling the touch of his fingers.

As Harry stretched and turned to get a better look, the left wing suddenly lifted and unfolded. It took a second to realize that he'd moved it himself. Without quite knowing how he'd done it, he'd somehow brought the wing tip forward where he could see it better. He tried it again, and there was a funny feeling like the pull of new muscles, or at least muscles moving in some new way, across his back and chest. He turned around and after a moment, he could make the other wing lift and spread itself, too.

Next he faced the mirror and concentrated on lifting both wings at once. There was a whoosh of air, a rustle of feathers, and his wings jumped out behind him into a huge tent of feathers that reached almost across the little room. Harry was so startled at the size of his wingspread that he relaxed quickly, and they dropped smoothly down to their narrow folded shape.

After a moment he tried it again, and this time, when the wings were up and spread, he decided to try bringing them down a little bit harder. They came down with a rush of wind, and for a moment Harry felt his feet lifted right off the floor.

It was all Harry could do to keep from shouting

"Whoopee!" right out loud. He could fly! He, Harry Houdini Marco, could fly like a bird! In a burst of enthusiasm he spread his wings and fanned them HARD! The rush of air blew the lamp off the table, sent the curtains fluttering out the window, and Harry's head went CRACK against the ceiling.

The next thing he knew he was sitting on the side of the bed rubbing the top of his head. It hurt like everything, and he could already feel a bump beginning to rise. Something else was hurting, but for a confused moment he couldn't figure out just what it was. Then he realized he was sitting on the end of one of his wings. He straightened it out behind him and the pain went away. At least that one did. But his head still hurt and his enthusiasm for flying seemed to be permanently damaged.

The longer he sat there and thought about it, the more discouraged he became. It really looked as if poor old Mr. Mazzeeck had goofed again. Of all the crazy things to give him. Him! Humpty Dumpty Harry, the guy who went around black and blue from one end to the other with nothing but feet and a bicycle to fall off of. And now he was going to fly. That was a good one! Way up in the sky, he'd be going maybe a hundred miles an hour, or more. Great! Just GREAT! And how was he going to look after he'd smashed into the Coit Tower, for instance, on some foggy night? Or gotten tangled up in some high tension electric wires?

And there was no use kidding himself. He was just the boy who could do it.

Magic and
Some Black and Blue

Harry's complete discouragement with flying didn't last very long. As a matter of fact, it really only lasted until the pain had faded from the bump on the top of his head. It left behind, though, a very vivid reminder of what Mr. Mazzeeck had said about proceeding with caution, and of his own promise to be careful.

After his head began to feel better, he got up and went to his window. He leaned out and looked into the foggy night. Below, fading away down the hill, were street lights and the lights of houses, blurred and pale through the drifting fog. To climb out on his window sill and take off into the blinding mist would be stupid, to say the least. He'd have to think of a safer place to learn.

Just then, he noticed the roof of the Furdells' carriage house and he knew right away where it was going to be. He got out his flashlight, the extra big one that Mr. Brighton had given him for his birthday, and cautiously opened the door of his room. Marco's Boarding House slumbered in an after-midnight kind of quietness. On the stairs, Harry kept close to the wall, where the old boards were less likely to squeak. When he reached the ground floor hall, he headed for the kitchen and the back door; and made a short dash through the foggy yard to the carriage house.

Once inside, Harry stopped to catch his breath and turn on his flashlight. There were overhead lights, but it would be a risk to turn them on. One of the windows faced the house and too much light might bring someone to investigate. At night, the carriage house had always seemed a spooky place to Harry. Even with the lights on, the immensely high ceiling where the hayloft used to be was full of shadows. But tonight, Harry wasn't a bit frightened. Somehow, having wings made a difference.

Except for Lee Furdell's beat-up old Oldsmobile, the carriage house was empty, so there was plenty of floor space. Harry walked to one end of the building, grasped his flashlight firmly in both hands and spread his wings.

At first he didn't try to go very far or very high. He fanned his wings hard, took off, and tried stopping right away. He soon learned that a quick run forward helped him to get under way, and that in order to stop, all he needed to do was make huge cups of his wings to catch the air. The cupped wings slowed him up and at the same time acted as kind of parachutes to bring him down easily. Once or twice he didn't come down quite easily enough to keep himself from collecting a couple of new reminders to "proceed with caution." One time it was a skinned knee, and another a bruised heel.

When he finally felt ready to try it from one end of

the barn to the other he made a marvelous discovery. He found that once he was really under way his body leveled out into a kind of swimming position with his toes trailing along behind. When that happened, the flying became much easier. Balancing, which had been a problem before, was suddenly almost automatic, and he no longer had to beat the air frantically to stay up. Once his body leveled out, it took only long gentle strokes to keep him gliding smoothly through the air.

From one end of the barn to the other he went, over and over again, getting more confident with every flight. He kept at it until it was perfect. Two or three fast hard beats to get air-borne and leveled out, and then a swooping, breath-taking glide to the far wall. Once there, he simply cupped his wings, back pedaled, and came down gently, feet first. Finally, he got so confident that he tried a quick pin-point landing on the roof of the Oldsmobile. He came down perfectly, feather-light, and right in the middle of the roof. And that made him so confident, that he decided to fly straight up and land on the huge crossbeam, high up under the roof of the barn.

That was nearly a mistake. In the first place, there were spiders' webs up there, which wasn't very pleasant. Harry brushed the sticky clinging webs off his face and chest, and shook them off his wings and got ready to leave in a hurry. That was when the dumb thing happened. As he looked down his flashlight beam, down, down, through the shadows, he suddenly froze. It wasn't too surprising. After all, Harry had only had wings for maybe an hour or an hour and a half, and for almost twelve years he'd had a lot of painfully bad luck with high places. Spiders' webs, or no spiders' webs, he sat down quickly on the crossbeam and grabbed hold with both hands.

There he sat for several minutes, shaking like crazy, with his wings trailing helplessly down on each side of the crossbeam. He tried to tell himself that he knew how to fly, and jumping off wasn't any different from taking off from the ground; but it wasn't any use. Not until he got to thinking what it would be like to have everybody come in the morning and find him up there, did he get up nerve enough to try again. He stood up, unfolded his wings, shut his eyes and jumped. And the moment he was in the air again, he wasn't afraid at all. He came down in a wonderful gliding spiral. It was better than anything he'd tried yet.

After that, he practiced a few more spirals until he got the knack of slanting his wings into a turn, and knew just how much to slant to sharpen a turn, or smooth it out. Then he felt ready to go outdoors.

In the tiny back yard Harry looked around him and up into the sky. There was certainly no room for a running take-off and he would have to climb very steeply. He would be fanning his wings very hard—if he could make it at all—just as he was going past the windows of the boarding house. The motion or the rustle of feathers might bring someone to the window.

It was just about then that he thought of the perfect take-off spot—the flat roof of the carriage house. He could take off away from the buildings on Kerry Street and over the roof of the houses on the street below.

He ducked back into the Furdells' yard and climbed

the outside stairway to the roof. Once there he stopped for a minute to look and listen. All the windows in the boarding house were dark; and in the Furdells' house, only one small light was on somewhere on the second floor. There was no sound but the far-away honking of car horns, and no movement except the slow drift of the fog. At last, Harry took a deep breath, spread his wings, and took off into the blinding fog.

Up and up he went, in a wide circle, his heart pounding with a crazy excitement that was more than half fright. The wind was wet against his face and his ears were full of the breathy whirr of feathers. It was a pretty frantic and frightening few minutes until at last he broke out above the fog into the clear open starlit sky.

Coming up so suddenly out of damp gray blindness, Harry was amazed to see how bright it was, and how clearly he could see. As he climbed higher into the starlit brightness the fog became only a rolling gray river beneath him. It poured in through the Golden Gate in great gray billows, spread out over the water of the bay, and spilled up onto the surrounding land. To the south, the tops of some of the tallest buildings looked like the last remains of a sunken city. As Harry turned in his circling flight, he caught a glimpse of the twin towers of the Golden Gate Bridge, barely showing above the foggy flood. Farther north, small patches of the hills of Marin could be seen through the fog breakers that dashed over their tops and almost seemed to splash down to the bay below.

As Harry went on climbing up and up he suddenly noticed a wonderful feeling of warmth. The air above the fog blanket was a whole lot warmer than it had been further down. It was the good feel of sudden warmth that made Harry realize how cold he'd been for a long time. All that time in the carriage house he must have been freezing, but he'd been too excited to notice. He decided right then that flying around San Francisco without a shirt wasn't a good idea.

The warm air above the fog blanket was so comfortable, and the fog-flooded world beneath him was so fascinating that Harry stopped being even the least bit afraid. In fact, for a few minutes he came close to forgetting where he was and what was keeping him up there. Without intending to, he had been flying slower and slower. It all came back as quick as anything, though, when he suddenly started to fall.

Right then Harry learned two things in a hurry. If you fly too slowly you begin to sideslip—and you only make things worse by panicking and trying to climb too steeply. His feet dropped down and he began to slide backwards and downwards toward the water of the bay. It wasn't until he had spun through a heart-stopping tail spin, and several hundred feet of air, that he managed to get his balance back and catch the wind under his wings. With a huge gulp of relief, he started back up to the warm upper air. After that he kept his mind strictly on his flying.

Not that he didn't have any more trouble, because he did. Once when he tried to turn too quickly, and again when he first tried to soar, he lost his balance and started to fall. But he wasn't quite as frightened as he'd been the first time so it was easier to relax and let his body level out. Once he did that, his wings just naturally did the rest.

As time passed and Harry flew and flew and flew, he forgot all about the fog, the city below him, and just about everything. Nothing in the world seemed to matter but wings, and sky, and motion. The free and endless kind of motion that people are always looking for in a hundred different ways.

Flying was the way a swing swoops up; and the glide down a slide. It was the shoot of a sled downhill without the long climb back up. It was the very best throat-tightening thrills of skis, skates, surfboards and trampolines. Diving boards, merry-go-rounds, Ferris wheels, roller coasters, skate boards and soap-box coasters. It was all of them, one after the other, all at once and a thousand times over.

Harry didn't have any idea how much time had passed when, during a long quiet glide, he noticed that the sky above the Berkeley hills had turned the pale green color that it often was just before dawn. Morning wasn't far away. The thought brought Harry back to earth with a jolt. Mentally anyway. How to get back was the problem.

As he slanted into a sharp turn and a long slow glide towards home, he realized that it wasn't going to be easy. By taking his bearings from the bay and the hills and the few tall buildings that stuck up through the fog, he would be able to come down in the general vicinity. But it wasn't very likely that he would be able to go straight down to his own back yard. And it certainly wouldn't do to blunder around blindly looking for

Kerry Street. He'd be sure to wind up wrapped around a trolley line or tangled in telephone wires.

For a minute or two he felt panicky, but then he managed to calm down enough to think it over carefully. He drifted in a big circle over the general area of home and tried to figure something out. He finally decided to make as good a guess as he could, and go straight down and land. If he could hit a roof top, even if it wasn't too near home, it would be a good place to get his bearings without being seen, and then plan his next move.

He picked his spot carefully. Fortunately the fog had begun to thin a bit, and more buildings and hilltops were visible. Twin Peaks were in the clear now, and the towers of the bridge reached high above the fog. Harry located a tall apartment building that looked like one he could see from his own window, and if the blinking green glow to his left was what he thought it was—the drive-in just two blocks from home—he wasn't going to be far wrong. He cupped his wings just a bit and started down in as small and slow a spiral as he could manage. Once inside the fog belt he was blind and helpless. Straining his eyes until they hurt, and with his heart thumping in his throat, he drifted down and down until suddenly a dark surface rushed up beneath him. Desperately, he reversed his wing beat, but it was too late to keep from landing with a thud that sent him to his hands and knees.

"Ouch," he said, and then, "Oh, for Pete Squeaks!" He'd torn a big hole in the knee of his pajama pants. Mom wasn't going to like that. He stood up and looked around. Now that he was down, there was some reflected glow in the air from the street lights, and he could tell that he was on the flat roof of a large building. By some rare good fortune, he had come down in a rather small open area between a long clothesline and a very fancy T.V. antenna. A little bit more to one side or the other and he'd have messed up somebody's wash or else their T.V. reception. Not to mention what it might have done to him.

All of a sudden he realized that there was something familiar about the whole thing. He made his way carefully to the edge and looked over, and sure enough, there, right next door, was Marco's Boarding House. Harry had come down right smack dab on top of Madelaine's School of Ballet.

The rest was easy. He walked along the edge of the roof until he was exactly opposite his own window on the third floor. From there it took only a couple of flaps of his wings to take him across the alley. Of course, he did get sort of jammed in the window for a moment, because he forgot to fold his wings before he tried to go through. But he got them down all right and climbed into the room, with nothing more than a few splinters from the window frame. He felt pretty lucky about that, because he'd thought for a second that he was going to fall out again, backwards.

Because he'd made a few whacking and thudding noises getting into the room, he didn't waste any time about saying the reverse incantation. It wouldn't do to have Mom come in to investigate before he got rid of his wings. The incantation worked fine. The feeling wasn't quite as violent as when the wings grew. It was more of a shrinking sensation. The dizziness came down like a dark curtain and, when it was over, the wings were gone.

Harry couldn't help having a feeling of loss—a sharp stab of regret—even though he knew that his wings had to go for the time being, at least. He reached back suddenly and touched the spot where the wings had been. As he ran his fingers across his back, he had a strange sensation that in some unexplainable way the wings were still there. As if he would always be able to feel them there, now that he knew about them—deep inside his back, tiny wings or maybe only wing buds. Probably they'd always been there. Maybe everybody had wing buds, or at least the possibility of wings, only they just didn't know it. Maybe people had really been meant to have wings.

All of a sudden Harry realized that he was shivering violently. It had been very cold coming down through the fog belt, and it wasn't much warmer in his room. He pulled on his pajama top and then his robe for good measure, and jumped into bed.

Only a few hours later Harry woke up in a glorious glow of sunshine and excitement. He had extremely stiff shoulder muscles, a bump on his head, two skinned knees, a bruised heel, several splinters, torn pajama pants, and the beginnings of a cold in the head. Not to mention the most marvelous, wonderful, super-colossal secret in the whole world.

Harry's Flying Suit

It didn't turn out to be such a very bad cold in the head, at least not right at first. But it was bad enough to make Harry decide he ought to wear something more than pajama pants the next time he went flying. He'd have to pick out something to fly in—something light and yet warm. It wasn't until he slipped out of bed and was standing in front of his closet that he realized he had a problem: how do you get into a sweat-shirt when you're already wearing wings? Of course, you can cut some big holes for the wings to come through, but then you have a different problem: how to explain two big holes in the back of your sweat-shirt to Mom.

Harry was still standing in front of the closet trying to figure out what he could wear when Mom came in. "Hi," she said, "do you know what time it is?"

Harry looked at his clock on the bed table. "For Pete Squeaks!" he said. "It's nine o'clock. I slept right through breakfast."

"I called you earlier," Mom said. "But you didn't wake up. Then I remembered you were up late helping Mr. Mazzeeck move out, so I let you sleep in."

Up late! Mom didn't know the half of it. She'd flip if she knew how late he'd really been up. And what if she knew how far up?

Not that Harry wouldn't have liked to tell Mom all about it. But of course, he couldn't; he'd promised Mr. Mazzeeck to keep it a secret.

"Well, get dressed and come on down to the kitchen," Mom said. "I'll fix you some breakfast." She started to leave, but then she stopped and took another look. "Well, for goodness sake. What happened to your pants?" She was looking at the big hole that Harry had torn in the knee of his pajamas when he lit on the roof of Madelaine's School of Ballet.

"I guess I . . . Well, I just fell down," Harry said. It was certainly the truth, too, as far as it went. As long as Mom didn't start asking "where?" and "how come?"

He needn't have worried, though. Mom only shook her head slowly and went on out the door. After all, she'd known Harry long enough to know he usually didn't have any particular reason for that sort of thing.

But this morning Harry didn't waste any time brooding about the boring old subject of his clumsiness. He had better things to think about. Remembering about last night was almost as exciting as living it had been. In fact, every time he thought about what it had been like last night, up there over the city, he felt as if something had just pulled up a draw string on his stomach. He kept thinking about it all the time he was eating his breakfast at the kitchen table. Or trying to eat it anyway.

All of a sudden Mom said, "Harry, are you getting sick? You've hardly eaten anything and you have the strangest expression on your face. And you're sneezing, too. Three times since you came downstairs."

Harry did his best to convince Mom that he felt all right, and then he made a real effort to act normal while he finished his breakfast. He managed to eat two eggs and three bowls of cereal, which wasn't quite as much as usual, but close enough so that Mom stopped worrying.

As soon as his morning chores were finished, he went up to the attic. It had occurred to him that among the old clothes and costumes and things Mom kept stored up there, he might find something that would make a good flying outfit.

Inside the attic door, Harry couldn't help checking on the poster of the old Swami. It was still there, all right, behind the washstand, looking pale and dusty and not the least bit talkative. Harry grinned at himself sheepishly, and started in on his search.

It had been quite a while since he had looked through Dad's things. When Harry unfastened the latches and pushed back the lid of the big trunk the first thing he saw was Dad's high black hat and the ebony wand with the silver tip.

Right away he started feeling uncomfortable. Looking at all that stuff of Dad's made him feel—well, sad, of course—but something that was almost worse. Time can soften sadness until it's only a gentle ache, full of warm memories. But a guilty conscience is always sharp and cold. And that's what Harry felt every time he looked at the things Dad had tried to teach him to use. Dad had counted so much on his becoming a famous magician, and for a long time now he hadn't even tried.

Everything he found brought back memories. There were the little round disks that Dad could make appear and disappear between his fingers, or even into and out of his mouth and ears. That was a hard one to learn. Harry used to drop the things all over the floor, and once when he was trying the mouth trick, he'd darn near choked on one of the disks.

He sighed and put the stuff back into the trunk. There was no use even thinking about it. In spite of Dad's plans and the prophecy and everything else, he just wasn't ever going to be any good at magic.

"Wait a minute" Harry said, right out loud. Maybe the prophecy never meant that he was supposed to be a magician at all. The Swami had only said, "The boy has a rare gift and his magic will be of a very special kind." Suppose the rare gift meant Mr. Mazzeeck's gift of the silver bottle, and the special kind of magic just might be WINGS! If that was what it meant maybe he hadn't messed up the prophecy after all. Harry caught himself glancing over at the poster, as if he expected the Swami to let him know if he were on the right track. He wasn't exactly surprised to find that the poster Swami still wasn't talking. But anyway Harry felt a lot better about the whole thing.

He went back to looking through the trunk, but when he came to Dad's costumes he realized right away that they wouldn't do for flying. They were just too nice to cut holes in, and there wasn't a single one that had a place for wings to come through.

Next, he went through some boxes of old clothing,

but everything either didn't fit or wasn't warm enough to do any good. He was about to give up in the attic when he found a pair of old white drapes. They weren't what he'd had in mind, but they just might do.

The rest of the day Harry spent waiting around for night to come, and wishing he dared to fly in the daytime. But he knew it would be far too risky. Somebody might see him, and even if he was willing to risk losing his wings himself, it wouldn't be right to take a chance because of Mr. Mazzeeck.

While he waited for the long afternoon to be over, he talked to Lee Furdell for a while over the back fence. Lee said he'd been thinking about the Marriage Plan, but so far he hadn't come up with anything definite. He did think, however, that it would help if they could get rid of Miss Clyde, somehow.

"She doesn't show any signs of being dissatisfied with the boarding house, does she?" he asked.

"Gosh no!" Harry said. "She's happy as a clam. With Mom's good cooking and Mr. Brighton to flop her eyelashes at, she'll probably be here until the end of the world."

"Hmm!" Lee said. Then his sad brown eyes lit up with a twinkle. "I don't suppose you could manage to throw a medicine bottle at *her* ankle?"

Harry laughed. "I would if I could think of a way to do it that wouldn't look fishy. But even if I did, I bet it wouldn't work. It'd take a lot more than that to scare old Clarissa away."

"Well, I'll keep working on it," Lee said. "Maybe

I'll hit on a plan."

After dinner that night, Mom and Mr. Konkel and Mr. Brighton and Miss Clyde started a bridge game. There wasn't anything Harry could do about that, and besides it was better than having them split up, two and two, the wrong way. So he told everyone good-night and went on upstairs to his room. It was still pretty light outside, but he decided to get all ready so he could take off the minute it was dark enough to be safe.

He had a sneaking suspicion that he shouldn't fly at all tonight when he was already catching a cold; but he just couldn't wait any longer. Besides, if he dressed up nice and warm, it shouldn't do him any harm.

Some old white gym shoes would be nice and light for flying and at the same time keep his feet warm, and a pair of Levis would be much warmer than the thin pajama pants. Next, he was ready for his wings. He took off his shirt and got the silver bottle out from its hiding place at the back of his sock drawer.

His heart was thumping hard as he poured the glowing drops of ointment onto his shoulders, and his hands shook just a bit as he rubbed it in. He took a deep breath and recited the incantation:

> *Wing feather, bat leather, hollow bone,*
> *Gift of Icarus and Oberon,*
> *Dream of the earthbound—Spin and Flow*
> *Fledge and Flutter and Fan and GO!*

Again, there was the tingling, the violent sensation in his back and shoulders, and the whirling dizziness;

except that this time it wasn't quite so frightening. And then, there were the wings, just as huge and beautiful and terrific as he remembered them. And with the wings there came again the tremendous surge of pride, and a happiness as if a million dreams had come true, all at one time and place.

It was a while before Harry was able to get his eyes and mind off the wings themselves, and back onto the problem at hand—a good flying suit. The next step, once he got his mind back on it, was to figure out how he could use the drapes he'd found in the attic. They were a little dingy now, but they had once been white and they were made of a very thick material. They were all lined with something nice and soft, and at the ends there were fringes of stuff that looked like little tassels.

Harry tried several different ways of draping himself before he hit on the one that seemed to work the best. He finally hung one drape over his left shoulder, passed it behind, under his right wing, and across his chest in front. Then he pinned it several times down his right side. He draped the other one over his right shoulder and fixed it in the same way on the other side. The white rope-like belt from his bathrobe, tied around his waist, pulled it all together in the middle. When he was all through, the drapes made a neat criss-cross on his chest and back, and the fringy stuff hung down almost to his ankles. It looked okay in an old-fashioned way—like an ancient Roman, maybe, or somebody out of the Bible.

Of course, it wasn't much like what Harry had had in mind when he first started thinking about a flying

costume. He'd had a picture, in his mind's eye, that was more like—well, like a cross between an astronaut's gear and a skin diver's wet suit. But the drapes were warm at least, and since no one was going to see him anyway, it really didn't matter much what he looked like.

When Harry was all dressed and ready to go, he sat in the window of his room and thought about his plans for the evening. He watched lights come on across the bridge, and the water of the bay turn from dark blue to black. A few wisps of fog drifted in from the Golden Gate but most of the sky was clear and starry. It was going to be a great night for flying.

When the last twilight glow was gone, Harry tip-toed down the back stairs. He had thought about taking off from the window of his room, but he'd decided against it. Flying through a three-foot-wide window is a bit tricky when your wing span is around ten feet. Of course, you could just jump out with your wings folded, and hope you remembered how to get them working before you hit the ground. But after some consideration Harry had decided to stick with the carriage house roof as a take-off site. At least until he'd had a little more experience.

On the roof of the Furdells' carriage house there was room for him to fan his wings, slowly at first and then harder. It wasn't until then that he began to be sure he remembered what he had learned about flying the night before. He became more confident with each strong sweep of his wings; but before he took off, he stopped long enough to remind himself firmly to concentrate and to keep his mind on his flying. That was a lesson he wasn't going to forget again. Then he spread his wings, leaped up and out, and he was off, into a clear starry sky.

Monkey Island

Harry started his second flight in a mood of efficiency and confidence. Right away he accomplished something very important. It had occurred to him while he was sitting in his window waiting for the darkness to be complete, that he should take advantage of the clear sky and map out a landing route for foggy nights.

So when he took off from the carriage house roof that night, he climbed upward only until he felt he was out of sight from below. Then he leveled out and drifted in a large circle above Kerry Street, and made mental notes of everything he could see. He located the roof of Furdells' carriage house, and hovering directly above it, he picked out everything around that he might be able to see, above or through a deep fog.

It isn't easy to memorize angles and distances, but Harry gave it his full attention until he was sure he could zero in on the roof no matter how foggy it might be. On the next foggy night, he wasn't going to have to trust to guesses or dumb luck. When he finally took off on the next part of his flight plan, he was feeling proud of himself for thinking so far ahead.

Earlier in the day when Harry was making plans for the evening, he had decided on a visit to the zoo. Fleishhacker Zoo had always been one of his favorite places, and it occurred to him that it would be fun to find out what it was like at night. He'd have the whole place to himself, with no crowds in front of his favorite animals; and all the nocturnal animals that were usually asleep when you saw them, would be up and prowling around. It ought to be great.

Harry was feeling fine and flying strongly as he headed southwest towards Twin Peaks. Once he passed the peaks he ought to be able to see all the way to the beach and Fleishhacker Zoo. The wind was clean and sharp against his face, but his drapery robe was thick and warm. He liked the sound the drape fringe made whipping madly against the legs of his Levis. It was a keen high-speed sound, something like a playing card makes on the spokes of a bike wheel. The beat of his wings was strong and sure against the lifting wind, and up here in the open sky flying seemed to have become almost automatic.

As he approached Twin Peaks, he had to climb again in order to clear their tops; and the view from that height was so tremendous that he decided to go even higher to find out just how much he could see, all at one time. He began to spiral up and up until he was almost out of breath. At last he leveled out and drifted in a great circle high above Twin Peaks. Below him the whole bay area lay spread out in patterns of golden haze, midnight blue, and velvety black. Glittering streams of light bordered the darker patches, or laced in and out among them, like velvet embroidered with diamonds. To the west, the Pacific Ocean framed the white beach with an even whiter border of surf.

As Harry's slowly circling flight turned his face eastward, he could see the entire bay, stretching its dark arms far to the north and south, crossed only by the bridges in three thin bracelets of light. Directly across the bay, crowds of tiny lights climbed the lower slopes of the Berkeley hills, whose dark crests made a black border for the eastern sky.

It was just about the most beautiful sight Harry had ever seen. Below him lay San Francisco, the city that people said was the most beautiful place in the world, spread out like a gigantic living map. As he circled slowly he kept picking out familiar places. Some of them he recognized immediately, even though he generally saw them from a very different angle. Others were puzzling at first, and didn't seem to be quite where they belonged.

The Embarcadero with its fringe of piers was unmistakable, and so was the Ferry Building, Market Street and the huge glowing dome of City Hall. But Coit Tower seemed a lot nearer the bay than he would have expected, and the Golden Gate Bridge seemed farther to the west.

If he hadn't already made other plans, Harry could have stayed up there for hours. But the zoo ought to be great, too, so he finally turned toward the south and west and slanted into a long downward glide. As he passed over the dark treetops of Stern Grove, he was flying fairly low again, and it was only a few minutes later that he skimmed silently above the empty parking strip and the high fence that surrounded the zoo.

It had been quite a long flight for a beginner, and his wings were feeling a little tired. He was just thinking about finding a nice safe landing spot—it wouldn't do to land in the lions' grotto, for instance—when, just ahead of him, he saw a familiar sight. Monkey Island.

Monkey Island had always been one of Harry's favorite places at Fleishhacker Zoo. There are no bars at all around the island, only a small moat. There is a big hill of artificial boulders, with a waterfall coming down one side, and lots of nooks and crannies for sleeping and shelter. At one end of the island there is a good sandy beach where the monkey families sit around and sun themselves on nice days and the little babies play tag and scoot around on their stomachs in the sand, just like real kids. Near the beach, at the edge of the moat, there is a dead tree. It isn't much more than a slender trunk going straight up like a telephone pole; but the monkeys like to play on it.

Anyway, the island was one of the places that Harry liked most, and that was probably the reason he did what he did. If there had been time to stop and think it over, he might have had better sense, but there wasn't any time at all. He was on the island almost before he knew what was happening.

It was one of his best landings. His scooping wings caught the ocean breeze, and he came down beautifully, feet first, right on top of the little hill. There he was, standing right at the top of Monkey Island's hill, with the little waterfall trickling down from just below his feet. Everything was very quiet and peaceful, and although it was darker than up in the open sky, there was plenty of light for him to see his way around. Harry was just thinking that the monkeys were probably asleep in the little caves and crannies and wondering if he'd get to see them at all when, suddenly, the little hill erupted like a monkey volcano.

In a split second the whole island was jumping with shrieking monkeys, and more seemed to be oozing out of every crack in the hill. The screeching and chattering was so unnerving that Harry couldn't think what to do. It seems like anybody would know that there's not much point in arguing with a bunch of hysterical monkeys, but for a minute all Harry could think to do was say, "Shhh! Be quiet! I'm not going to hurt anything. Hush up, won't you? Oh, for Pete Squeaks shut up!"

It was just about then that a particularly loud noise from right behind him made Harry look back over his shoulder. A great big monkey was dashing up the hill yelling like crazy, in an especially nasty tone of voice. He was heading right for Harry's ankles. Instantly Harry decided not to wait to see if a monkey could bite clear through Levis, gym socks and drapery fringe. He took off straight ahead, without even fanning his wings first to warm up.

Everything might have been fine if Harry's mind had been on his flying, but it's pretty hard to concentrate with a screaming monkey hanging on to the tail of your drapery. And that's exactly what the monkey was doing. The crazy monkey had gotten himself so worked up over being a hero for all the lady monkeys, by chasing off the intruder, that when Harry took off, the monkey jumped after him and grabbed him by the robe. He was still hanging there and yelling when Harry ran into the dead tree.

In the excitement and semi-darkness, Harry didn't even see the tree until he was almost on it. He just had time to throw out his hands to ward off a head-on collision. As his hands grabbed hold of the narrow trunk, worn smooth by many monkey hands, his momentum carried the rest of him on around the tree, like—well, like a monkey on a string. Only, in this case, it was more like two monkeys—Harry and the real one, who was still hanging on to the other end of Harry.

Whatever happened next was so quick and confused that Harry never did remember it very clearly. He did recall a couple of jarring thumps, and a sudden coldness, and the next thing he knew he was sitting in the middle of the moat and a wet monkey was sitting right beside him.

The monkey wasn't yelling any more. The cold water must have shocked all the hero business right out of him, because he scrambled for the island side of the moat almost as fast as Harry scrambled for the other. Harry was just trailing his wet wing-tips over the railing, when through the yelling of the monkeys, he heard something else. It was the sound of running feet and a human voice shouting something. Harry glanced around frantically and scurried for the nearest bushes. There wasn't time to take off and even if there had been, he was sure he couldn't get two feet off the ground, with his wings all wet and his drapes heavy with water.

He had barely crouched down under the bushes, when a man appeared, running down the walk with a flashlight in his hand. When the watchman reached the moat, he stood at the railing for a long time, shining his light around on the island, where the monkeys were beginning to quiet down. Meanwhile Harry crouched under the bushes, dripping and shivering. He had just about decided that he really was going to freeze clear to death, when he saw something that scared him so much he forgot all about the cold.

The watchman had started to walk slowly around the island shining his flashlight from side to side as he went. And it was just at that moment that Harry noticed the trail of water that led from the edge of the moat directly to his hiding place. As a matter of fact, there were three trails, a big wide one in the middle and a little narrow one on each side where the water had run off the tips of his wings. In just a minute, the watchman would reach those trails, and when that happened, Harry knew he had better be somewhere else.

As quickly and quietly as he could, he began to move away from his hiding place. By making use of a tree, a trash can, and a bench, he had scurried and ducked part way around the island by the time the watchman came to the place where the trail of water left the moat.

Peeking out from behind the bench, Harry saw the watchman stop as his flashlight beam hit the trail of dribbled water, and saw him follow the trail backward to the edge of the moat. Near the railing he stopped and seemed to be picking something up off the ground.

As the watchman held his find under the beam of the flashlight to examine it, Harry was able to see it, too. He wasn't positive, but it looked a lot like a feather, a great big white feather.

The watchman turned and followed the trail of water to the bushes, where Harry had just been hiding. He tramped around in the underbrush for a moment, and then came out carrying another feather. For a while, he just stood there, looking at the feathers, and then he began to shine his light up into the branches of the nearby trees.

As the watchman moved slowly back the way he had come, this time searching the treetops, Harry scooted away from the bench and down the path that led to the flamingo pond. On the hill above the pond he found a hidden place where there was enough room to flutter his wings hard, to shake the water out of them. At first they felt heavy and awkward, and water flew in every direction; but after a few minutes of fluttering they seemed to be back to normal. Just before he took off, Harry wrung out the tail ends of his drapes and emptied out his gym shoes.

There was still enough water in his drapes and wings to make the take-off more difficult than usual. He just barely managed to clear the treetops, but then he was off and away, on the long cold flight home. And was it ever cold! The cold ocean wind flapped his soggy drapes, and plastered his wet Levis against his legs. Harry didn't do any sight-seeing or fancy flying on that trip. All he could think about was flying hard and fast toward a warm dry bed.

It wasn't until he was home and had been in bed long enough to stop shivering, that he realized what had saved him from being caught. The watchman must have stopped searching the bushes and started in on the treetops because he thought Harry was a bird. He'd found the feather by the moat, and maybe he figured that some big white bird had landed in the water and scared the monkeys. Then he'd found the place where Harry had sat under the bushes. There must have been a puddle of water there and some more feathers. The watchman probably thought that the bird had rested there for a while before it flew off.

It occurred to Harry that there had been a lot of leaves under the bushes, so it wasn't likely that he'd left any footprints. Lucky for him that it hadn't been soft mud or sand. Lucky for Harry; and come to think of it, lucky for the watchman, too. After all, the zoo directors might be a little suspicious of a night watchman who reported a big white bird wearing gym shoes.

A Little More Believing

Harry didn't go flying again for five whole nights. The dunking in the monkey's moat and the long cold flight home hadn't been at all good for his cold. Or to put it more accurately, it had been fine for the cold, but it hadn't done Harry any good. He'd even had a fever for a day or two and that was really unusual, for him.

The whole thing was pretty boring. Mom made him stay in bed for two days, and even after he was feeling fine, he didn't dare go flying for fear Mom would come up to check on him at night. Whenever he was the least bit sick, Mom always came up to his room in the middle of the night to be sure he was all right. So he had to wait until he was sure Mom had finished worrying about the cold before he dared go on another flight.

On the fifth day Harry was pretty sure that Mom had stopped worrying, because she mentioned that it would be a good time for him to get caught up on his chores. So he mowed the lawn and swept the driveway, and went to the store for groceries. He even went further than usual and helped Mom with the washing.

Doing the washing wasn't one of Harry's regular chores, but he wasn't just doing a boy scout bit, when he offered to help. There was a special reason on that particular Monday. He just about had to get his flying-drapes washed before he used them again.

Five nights before, when he got back from falling in the moat, he had hung the wet drapes on a hook, way at the back of his closet. They had dried out finally, but they were all dingy and the fringe around the bottom was caked with mud. Besides, there was a strange sort of smell about them. Harry had never really minded the way monkeys smelled—at least, not as much as some people seemed to—but just the same, he thought, it wouldn't be a bad idea to get his drapes washed before he wore them again.

He managed to get the drapes in and out of the washing machine without Mom seeing them. Then he sneaked them up to the attic and hung them out on the line Mom kept up there for wet days. He was hanging the rest of the wash in the back yard, when Lee Furdell called to him from across the fence.

Lee wanted to know how things were, and if there had been any progress on the Plan. Harry felt a little ashamed when he realized that he hadn't thought much about it lately. After all, it was a good Plan and pretty important. Even though being able to fly was great, as far as Harry was concerned, it didn't do a thing for Mom. And it didn't change the fact that Mom had too much work and worry trying to make a living for them all by herself. Harry had to admit to Lee that things were pretty much the same and that he hadn't had any bright ideas for changing them.

"Well, I'm afraid I haven't either," Lee said. "But I do think that the first step is to get Miss Clyde to move out. From what you tell me, Hal won't have a chance to notice your mother as long as she's around. There ought to be something you could do, something harmless, of course, that would convince her that she wants to move." Then Lee laughed. You could always tell by his eyes when he was laughing, even though it never showed much anywhere else. "You don't suppose Miss Clyde is the type who believes in ghosts," he said. "Maybe you could make her think that Marco's is haunted."

"Hey," Harry said. "That's an idea. It looks kind of haunted, all right. I mean it's so dark and big and gloomy and everything." But on second thought he had to add, "I don't know, though. Miss Clyde looks to me like the kind of person who doesn't believe in ghosts or anything, much. You know what I mean?"

"I'm afraid I do," Lee said. "There are a great many people who are that way nowadays, more's the pity. A little more believing in things would do—"

At that point Lee broke off. Olive Furdell had come out on the back porch and was looking at them. There wasn't any time for Harry and Lee to pretend that Lee hadn't been "wasting his time on the neighbors" again. That's what Olive always accused Lee of doing. At least, that was one of the things. There were a lot of other things, and you couldn't help knowing what they were, because of the kind of voice Olive Furdell had. Every time Olive started accusing Lee of something, half the block knew about it right away.

But this time Olive didn't start yelling immediately. Instead she just came over to the fence where they were standing. She had a piece of white candy in her hand. "Leland," she said, "this is some of the divinity from that new recipe. I wanted to see what you thought of it before I made up a big batch." She broke the piece of candy in two and handed some over the fence to Harry. "Hello, Harry," she said, "I see you've been helping your mother with her washing."

Harry was so astounded that it took him a minute to remember to say thanks, even. Then, just as he popped the piece of divinity into his mouth, it occurred to him that maybe Olive had gone off her rocker, or something. She wasn't acting normal, that was for sure! So maybe the candy wasn't normal, either. What if she'd put something *really* different in it? Like rat poison, for Pete Squeaks!

He only worried for a second, though, because the candy tasted just great, and besides, Lee wasn't acting too surprised. He was just nibbling at his piece of candy thoughtfully with a tasting expression on his face. "It seems fine to me," he said at last. "Every bit as good as the old way, I'd say, and quite a bit easier to make. It seems to me that we ought to try it, at least for a while."

"Well, that's what I thought," Olive said. "But I wanted to see if you agreed. What do you think of it, Harry?"

"Think?" Harry stammered. "What do I th—Oh, I think it's fine. That's really great divinity, Mrs. Furdell."

"Thank you, Harry," Olive said. Then she just

turned around and went back into the house. She didn't even say anything to Lee about "when was he going to get back to work?" and that was just about her favorite question, where Lee was concerned.

After Olive Furdell disappeared into the house, Harry and Lee just stood there staring after her. Nobody said anything Harry was dying to ask some questions, but he didn't quite know how to do it. That is, he couldn't think of a way to ask that didn't sound sort of disrespectful.

At last, Lee turned back to Harry with a little sigh. He smiled his small quiet smile. "You look rather puzzled, Harry," he said. "I wish I could satisfy your curiosity, but I'm afraid I can't. I've been a bit bewildered myself lately."

"Oh, I wasn't curious or anything like that," Harry said. "I just—well—it sure was nice of Mrs. Furdell to bring us out that candy."

"Yes indeed. It certainly was." Lee looked back toward the house again and scratched his head. Then he shook it back and forth, slowly and thoughtfully. Finally he gave a little shrug. "Well, Harry," he said at last, "It's time I was getting back to the shop. But as I was starting to say, a little more believing in things would do this world a lot of good. You take all the believing out of life, and it doesn't leave much room to grow in." He started away toward the house, but then he stopped and turned back. "And take it from me, Harry, the unbelievable can happen almost anywhere."

An Angel!
For Pete Squeaks!

When darkness finally came that night, Harry knew exactly where he was going and what he was going to do when he got there. He'd done a lot of thinking during those five days that he'd been cooped up, and he'd come to an important decision. He was going to have to go somewhere where it would be safe to do some serious practicing. It would have to be a place where he could land and take off as much as he wanted and fly low where there were things to maneuver around.

He'd found out that flying low was the riskiest part about having wings, and it was the only part that he'd never really had a good chance to practice. Up in the open sky, things were much simpler, and besides, way up there you had a little time to correct a mistake if you made one. Down near the earth, there often wasn't any time at all. Like when that dead tree had appeared suddenly right ahead of him. If he'd only had a little more practice at such things, he might have been able to dodge it. And if he had been able to avoid the tree, he would also have avoided a real wowzer of a cold and a couple of king-sized bruises, besides.

Of course, bruises were old stuff to Harry; but with those two new big black and blue places, plus the ones he already had, it was beginning to look as if he were on his way to setting some kind of a record. Harry Marco —holder of the gold medal in bruise collecting!

There wasn't any doubt about it, the curse had really been working when Mr. Mazzeeck picked out wings as the right kind of magic for Harry. Mr. Mazzeeck had been so proud of the fact that his company didn't have anything to do with Black Magic, that it didn't seem likely they intended to hand out Black and Blue Magic, either. But mistake or no mistake, Harry knew he wouldn't have missed having wings for anything.

So when Harry took off from the carriage house roof that night he headed directly for Golden Gate Park. He knew of a nice lonely spot, not too far from the stadium, where there were lots of trees and bushes to maneuver around; and nice soft grass, in case he had an accident.

It was amazing how quickly he reached the eastern end of the park. Wings were really great when it came to getting some place in a hurry. Harry couldn't help thinking about the time he'd walked most of the way home from the park, on the day he'd first met Mr. Mazzeeck. He remembered how long it took and how tired he'd been. And tonight he'd covered the same distance in only a few minutes.

Steinhart Aquarium and the museums rushed past below him and only a minute or two later he came to the place he had in mind. He was pretty sure that no one would be in such a lonely part of the park after dark, but just the same, he didn't take any chances. He circled down slowly, lower and lower, looking carefully for any sign of life. Nothing was there but trees and bushes and dark stretches of smooth lawn.

So he began to practice. He did landings and take-offs at various speeds and from different angles. He flew close to the ground, gliding around trunks of trees and bushes. He swooped up into tall trees and came to a stop on sturdy branches. He even mastered a particularly exciting maneuver that allowed him to fly through a space that was too narrow for the full width of his out-stretched wings.

He found that if he saw a narrow space coming up ahead, a sudden spurt of speed would give him power enough to glide through with his wings partly folded, like the backswept wings of a supersonic plane. It was really terrific to shoot between two tree trunks almost on momentum alone, and then just as he burst out into the open, spread his wings and glide upward.

Of course, it wasn't really all that simple. That is, he didn't just do all those things perfectly the first time he tried them. As a matter of fact, his bruise collection, which had begun to fade a bit during his illness, acquired new and spectacular additions before the night was over. Not to mention, several twig scratches on his face and arms, and a big green streak down the front of his nice clean drapes.

He got the green streak when he was seeing just how low he could fly. He was skimming along over the lawn just a foot or two up, when a little rise took him by surprise. What happened next was a little like body surfing without any water. The grass was wet with dew and slippery, and Harry tobogganed along over it for quite a way on his stomach before he ran out of momentum. After he got his breath back he found that he wasn't hurt at all, except for a few tender ribs and the big grass stain down his front.

All in all, things went pretty well, and Harry discovered that by concentration and determination, he could do all sorts of things he hadn't thought possible. When he finally began to feel tired, he decided to head for home right away before he got careless and had an accident. But then, after being so sensible for once, he did something very stupid. Instead of climbing immediately to a safe flying altitude, he started off down through the park at low level. He was just telling himself that nobody in his right mind would be out in the park at that hour when, suddenly, somebody was.

Harry had just swooped out from between two trees, using his new supersonic plane technique. As he cleared the trunks and shot out into the open, he saw before him, and only a few feet below, something that made his heart pop up into his throat like a cork in a bottle. There was a sidewalk, with a bench beside it. Behind the bench was a glowing street lamp, and on the bench, staring straight at Harry, was a man. As Harry swept past the bench, he was so close he could see quite clearly the man's astonished, open-mouthed face. He'd seen Harry all right, there wasn't the shadow of a doubt about that.

Just across the small clearing there was a huge tree

with thick heavy foliage. Harry headed for the tree, and once safely hidden by its leaves he came to a quick stop on a strong branch near the trunk. He just clung there for a minute, holding on to the trunk of the tree and wondering desperately what was going to happen next.

He was afraid to go on flying towards home for fear his wings might drop off at any moment. Mr. Mazzeeck had said that if there was any "public notice" the gift would be taken away. Just what did that mean? He reached back quickly and touched his wings. He almost expected to find them gone; but at least for the moment, they were still there. If they'd been gone, he really would have been in a mess. Imagine being found in the morning stranded in the top of a tall tree, dressed in a pair of old drapes. Harry couldn't help shuddering at the thought.

But the wings didn't go away; and after he began to think more calmly, Harry decided Mr. Mazzeeck had probably meant there mustn't be a big fuss about the wings. Like getting into the papers and television, for instance.

It was just about then that he began to wonder if that man on the bench was the type that liked to get things put in the paper. Suppose he went rushing off to Herb Caen, or one of the other columnists who liked to write interesting things about San Francisco, with the hot tip that there was a boy with wings flying around Golden Gate Park.

Harry lay down on his stomach on the branch and started to squirm out to where he could get another look at the man on the bench. Sometimes you could get a pretty good idea of what a person was likely to do just by looking at him. If the man was still sitting under the street lamp, Harry would be able to take a good look without being seen again himself.

The man was still there when Harry parted the

leaves and peeked through. Except for turning a bit towards Harry's tree, he hadn't moved at all; and from the expression on his face, he might as well have been struck by lightning. In spite of his worries about losing his wings, Harry couldn't help grinning a little. The guy looked so absolutely flabbergasted.

All at once the man lurched to his feet and started moving toward the tree. He took only a few steps, and Harry felt more comfortable. He had seen people walk like that before, and most of them had been coming out of Hugo's Bar and Grill, across the street from Wong's Grocery. Harry looked closer and noticed a big paper bag sitting on the bench; it wasn't a bit hard to guess what that was.

The man came a few more unsteady steps toward Harry's tree and then suddenly stopped and sank down onto his knees. Very slowly his hands came up in front of his face, with the fingers all laced together. He stayed that way for quite a while. Now and then, when he turned his face just a bit so that the light from the street lamp fell on it, Harry could see that his lips were moving.

Harry was beginning to feel pretty uncomfortable —and it wasn't just from the hard branch under his stomach—when the man finally got back on his feet. He moved slowly back to the bench and picked up the paper bag. Then he just stood there holding the bag straight out in front of him and looking at it. At last he turned and marched with unsteady determination to a trash can a little way down the walk. Harry clearly heard the crash as the bag hit the bottom of the can.

The man turned back towards Harry's tree for a minute, raised his hand in a funny kind of salute, and then went on down the sidewalk. He was trudging away with a lop-sided sort of firmness, as he disappeared from view behind the next grove of trees.

On the flight home, at a good safe altitude, Harry had two ideas. The first one made him feel good, but the second was a little upsetting.

The first idea was that he didn't have a thing to worry about as far as getting in the newspapers was concerned. It was obvious what people would think if that man in the park started telling people about seeing a flying boy. The poor guy probably knew what they'd think, too, and it was a safe bet that he'd never tell a living soul.

The other idea was a very strange one. Harry didn't think of it all at once. He was flying along peacefully, when all of a sudden he began to wonder what the man thought he had seen. A flying boy was odd, sure, but the way the man had acted, it was almost as if he'd seen a flying ghost.

It wasn't until Harry got back to his room, that he really admitted to himself what had happened. He hung a towel over his lamp to dim the light, and then he stood off across the room and looked at himself in the mirror. It was true all right.

If you were far enough away to miss the crew cut and the green stomach, you really might think you'd seen an angel. An ANGEL! for Pete Squeaks!

Days that Flew By

The next few weeks were full of flying. During the days, Harry did his chores and then hung around waiting for night to come. He was always sleepy because of being up so much at night, so in the afternoons he usually took a nap.

It must have been the naps that first got Mom started worrying. Of course she had no idea how sleepy three or four hours of flying can make you; all she knew was that until that summer Harry hadn't taken a nap since he was two years old, except when he was sick. So she began asking questions about how he felt and watching him in a worried way.

For a while Mom seemed to think the naps had some connection with the vacation plans fizzling again. Once she suggested to Harry that they might still be able to go. It wasn't hard for Harry to prove that they really couldn't afford it. Boarding-house-size water heaters cost a lot of money; and even if Miss Clyde had taken Miss Thurgood's room, she hadn't exactly taken her place. One thing about Miss Thurgood, she had always paid her rent on time; Miss Clyde was turning out to be the type who handed out excuses more often than money. After Harry had done his best to convince Mom that he wasn't feeling bad about missing the trip, she admitted that he was right, that they really didn't have enough money.

But once a mother starts worrying, it spreads worse than a bad case of poison oak, and it wasn't long before Mom found something else to worry about. She decided that Harry ought to look up some old friends, or maybe make some new ones. Ordinarily that wouldn't have been such a bad idea, but under the circumstances Harry couldn't get too enthusiastic. The guys he liked best had all moved to the suburbs or even farther; and none of the ones he liked second-best lived close enough to visit without making a big deal out of it. And what with flying and everything it just seemed like too much of an effort.

Once, just to keep Mom happy, he did spend the afternoon with a kid named Robert, who lived just a few blocks away, but it wasn't much fun. The only thing Robert liked to do was play Monopoly and cheat; like snitching money out of the bank or slipping an extra house on his property. He had his own special rules about how cheating was fine as long as nobody saw you. Robert said his rules made the game more exciting, but compared to flying it didn't seem like fun at all.

Except for Mom's worrying, things at home weren't too bad. At least, as far as Harry could tell they weren't getting any worse. Miss Clyde was still monopolizing Mr. Brighton's time and attention every minute that he was at the boarding house, and Mom was still spending too much time talking to old Konkel. But there didn't seem to be much progress in the wrong direction. Nobody had reached the whispering and hand-holding stage; at least, not that Harry had seen.

As for flying—that was more terrific all the time. Ever since that night in the park when he had practiced so hard, there hadn't been so many bumps and bruises. For quite a while there weren't even any narrow escapes.

Harry had worked out a system for take-offs and landings that was fairly foolproof. Because it was risky to go traipsing through the house with his wings on in the early evening, he soon forced himself to learn how to take off from his window. He would squeeze himself through the small opening and then, balancing on the outside sill, fall forward into a gliding take-off. It worked all right because the drop of the hill made it possible for him to glide over the roofs of the Piper Street houses before he began his climb. But the falling forward part was pretty scary the first few times.

After a few tries, however, he gave up the thought of coming home by way of his window. He never seemed to be able to manage it without a dangerous thud when he lit and then a mad scramble to keep his balance on the narrow sill until he could squeeze himself inside. So he had to go on using the carriage house and Madelaine's roof as landing places. The carriage house stairs and Madelaine's fire escape both led quickly to the Marcos' back yard. Mom kept an extra key hidden on the back porch, so Harry simply let himself in the back door and tiptoed up the back stairs to his room. It was always very late by then so there wasn't much chance of meeting anyone in the hall or on the stairs.

In fact, there was only one little thing that worried Harry just a bit. That was the flowers on the carriage house roof. He first noticed them quite early in the summer. He came in one night from an especially long flight and landed on the roof, as usual. He was just about to go down the stairs when he noticed something strange. Over in the corner of the roof, against the railing, someone had set up a little table. On it was a small vase full of some sort of sweet-smelling flowers and a candle in a glass holder.

When he saw it, Harry didn't think it was too important. He just supposed that some neighborhood kids had been using the roof as a playhouse, as he had done himself, and had left some of their stuff behind. But after he got into bed that night, he started to do some second guessing.

For one thing, there weren't any neighborhood kids left, except for some very little ones who lived on Piper, the next street down. It was just possible that they could have gotten into the Furdells' yard by the back way, but it didn't seem very likely. And there was something else that was even harder to explain. He hadn't thought about it before, but he was pretty darn sure those flowers and things hadn't been on the roof when he flew over it as he took off. It didn't seem a bit likely that those little kids from Piper Street had been out there playing house in the middle of the night.

It was all very mysterious, so Harry just stopped landing on the carriage house roof for a while, except on foggy nights. He had to go on using it then because his other landing place, Madelaine's roof, was too dangerous when you couldn't see to avoid all the clotheslines, lounge chairs, and T.V. antennas. As time went by, he stopped worrying about the little table; but once when he landed on the roof, he thought the flowers in the vase looked fresh. In the dark and fog, though, he couldn't be sure.

Sometimes that summer when Harry swooped out and away from his bedroom window, he had a definite destination in mind, but often he only wanted to fly. Then his favorite direction was out towards the middle of the bay. Out there above the open water he could swoop and glide and dive and climb without having to think about anyone looking up and seeing him.

But other nights he felt like going some place in particular. It was wonderful to be able to go any place, in any direction, as long as it wasn't too far to get back before dawn. Once or twice on particularly foggy nights, he crossed the bay and kept on going until the fog and the Berkeley hills were behind him. On the other side of the hills it was clear and warmer. He drifted on and on, looking down on housing developments and then on farms and pastures, until he was almost to the foothills of Mount Diablo. He lit once or twice to rest on quiet hilltops, and once, without meaning to, he stampeded a herd of horses that happened to be grazing nearby.

Other times he went north, across the Golden Gate to Marin County. Once he found Mr. Brighton's farm, and circled around it thinking what a great place it was and how much fun it would be to live there. It was a clear bright night, and the moonlight made the big old two-story house and the little barn and corral look like something out of an old-fashioned picture. Harry could just picture himself saddling up a horse out by the barn. It was just too bad that a picture like that hadn't occurred to Mr. Brighton.

Once in a while, Harry flew around the city, too, but that always seemed more dangerous. For one thing, all the thousands and thousands of lights made a golden haze that penetrated far up into the sky, so that it was impossible to fly very low without taking a big risk. And on foggy nights there was always the danger of running into a tall building or a church spire or something. One night when he was feeling particularly daring, he landed right on the top of the Fairmont Hotel. By peeking over the edge he could watch the glass-walled observation elevator going down the outside of the building, and for a minute he had a terrific urge to fly down and press his face against the glass. Boy, wouldn't that give those people in the elevator a jolt—seeing a face looking in at them, up there, twenty stories above everything?

But, of course, he didn't do it. "Public notice" was what Mr. Mazzeeck had said he mustn't have, and if peeking in the Fairmont elevator didn't cause public notice, nothing would. Besides, he wouldn't want to give somebody a heart attack, or anything like that.

An Angel for Tommy

It was early in August that Harry decided to explore Alcatraz prison. The deserted old prison on its tiny island had always been a part of Harry's private view from his third-story window. But now it occurred to him that it might be interesting to see close up.

It had been a clear day; but as Harry began his climb above Kerry Street that night, he noticed the fog rolling in through the Golden Gate. The first wispy fingers were already circling the island of Alcatraz. By the time he arrived above it, the fog was drifting in thin ghostly veils past the high walls of the old prison. As Harry glided in a circle on silent wings, he could hear only a distant lapping of water and now and then the moan of a foghorn or the shrill cry of a gull.

Although he had planned to land and do a bit of exploring, Harry found suddenly that he had changed his mind. He told himself that there was probably a night watchman left on the island; but that wasn't the only reason. It was more a strange feeling he had that the island wasn't really deserted at all. The prisoners were all gone, but something had been left behind. It was as if the island were still alive with the misery and loneliness and despair that had lived there for so many years. Harry decided on some practice-flying up over the bay instead.

Harry's skin was still a little crawly as he turned north and headed away from Alcatraz, but by the time he reached Angel Island he was feeling more normal. He flew over the island and kept going up the bay. He practiced dives and figure eights and belly-rolls until he saw the camel-backed outline of the Richmond Bridge just ahead. Then he turned and headed for home.

On the way back he passed a place where some people were having a party on the deck of a yacht that was tied up to a pier. The fog was quite thick now, so Harry was able to land in the little crow's nest on the tallest mast, without any danger of being seen. But the deck was lit up so brightly with strings of colored lights, that he could see the people dancing, or just milling around talking and laughing. At first, it was fun to sit up there over their heads and spy on them, but after a while Harry decided it was a pretty boring party, so he went on.

Just a little way below the ship-party, when Harry was still flying quite low near the coast, he heard a strange sound. It seemed to come out of the fog from somewhere farther out in the bay, and at first Harry kept right on going because he was so sure that he must have imagined it. After all, why would a baby be crying somewhere out there on the dark lonely water. But then he heard it again.

Harry lifted his right wing and slid into a turn, out

towards the center of the bay. In a moment he heard the crying again and someone, it sounded like a very little kid, called, "Help!" Harry knew then that he wasn't just imagining.

The sobbing grew louder, and finally Harry saw them—two little tiny kids, adrift in a small plastic dory. As he coasted silently in a circle above them, he could see that the crying was coming from the littlest one, who lay all crumpled up in a heap on the bottom of the small rowboat. She didn't look much bigger than a baby, and she was wailing steadily in a hopeless, exhausted way. The other one was a boy, maybe four or five years old. He was sitting up on the seat and rowing, but with only one oar, and missing the water half the time at that. The rowing was only making the boat go in a small circle, but the tide was moving it, too; down the bay towards the Gate and the big ship traffic, and beyond that the waves of the ocean.

As Harry watched, the little boy stopped rowing and called, "Help!" again, but his tear-choked voice seemed to go no place at all in the muffling fog. He sat very still for a while as if listening, but except for the steady wailing from the baby on the floor, there was no sound but the far-off bellow of foghorns.

Harry's first thought was to go right down and land in the boat, but for once he thought again before he acted. For one thing he wasn't sure he could land on a little tiny boat like that without tipping it over, and even if he did manage, it would be even harder to take off again. It took quite a backwards kick to get air-borne, and the tiny dory didn't look as if it would be able to stand anything like that. And once in the boat, unable to take off again, Harry would be almost as helpless as the two little kids.

Besides, there was the "public notice" business. He had to find a way to help those kids without letting anybody see him, and that wasn't going to be easy.

After careful consideration, he was pretty certain there was only one safe way to do it. He would fly home just as fast as he could and make an anonymous phone call to the Coast Guard. Of course, it would be a little hard to tell them just where to look, what with the fog and the tide and all, but he could give them a pretty good general idea. Then, if the Coast Guard believed him, and if they got started right away—before the kids drifted in front of some big freighter, or got to moving around and tipped the boat over—

Just about then the one with the oar started talking to the smaller one on the bottom of the boat. "Don't cry, Donna," Harry heard him say. "See how hard I'm rowing, Donna. We'll be home in a few minutes. Don't cry any more."

That did it. He couldn't go off and leave a brave little kid like that; not with all that fog and tide and only one silly oar. "Public notice" or no "public notice," Harry dropped a little lower and yelled, "Hey kid, look up here!"

The little boy looked up. "Hi," he said, and then without even hesitating, "Are you an angel?"

The question might have been more of a jolt if Harry hadn't gotten a little used to the idea already. So he just yelled back, "Yeah, I'm an angel. And I've come to help you get home."

The little boy didn't say anything for a minute, but Harry could see his turned-up face, a pale oval in the dim foggy light. "That's good," he said at last. "I was getting tired. And Donna won't stop crying. And we're all wet 'cause the oar splashes." His voice began to quaver, "And it's awful cold."

"Well, everything's okay now," Harry called. "We'll have you home in a flash. But don't start crying. You may have to help out."

The little boy wiped his face. "What are you going to do?" he asked.

That was just it. Harry didn't know what he was going to do. He didn't dare land, and he wasn't at all sure he could fly carrying anything as heavy as the boy, and he certainly couldn't carry them both at once. "Why don't you come down?" the boy called.

"I think I'm too big for your boat," Harry yelled back. "But don't worry. I'll think of something." He circled some more, trying to come up with an idea, but all he decided was that the kids didn't need a fake angel, they needed a real one.

While Harry worked on the problem of just what a fake angel could do, since there wasn't a real one around, the little boy got on his knees on the seat and reached for something off the front end of the boat. "Hey, sit down!" Harry shouted. "Do you want to fall out?"

When the boy sat back down, he had a rope in his hand; a rope that was attached to the front end of the boat. "Could you pull us home by our rope?" he asked.

Well, for Pete Squeaks! The kid had more sense than he did. "Yeah, sure," Harry said.

He had the boy sit on the bottom of the boat and hold the end of the rope up as high as he could with one hand. "And as soon as I grab the rope, you lie down flat by your sister," Harry said, "because there may be a jerk. And stay there until I tell you."

Then Harry made a big turn and came in as slowly and as close to the water as he dared. As he passed over the boat, he reached down with one hand and grabbed. There was an awful jerk when Harry caught the end of the rope. The boat almost stood on its tail, and Harry thought for a second that he was going to take a nose dive into the water. But the kid had done what he was told, and he didn't fall out. When Harry got himself leveled out again and looked back, he could see the two of them lying there as the dory sped through the foam like a motorboat.

It was pretty scary flying so close to the bay. If just one wing tip dipped too low and hit the water, he'd be sure to lose control, and that would be that—not only for Harry, but for the little kids, too. So he concentrated harder than he ever had before, and in a few minutes he saw the dark foggy outline of the shore.

He turned just a bit and followed the shore line until he saw some lights shining dimly through the fog and then the outline of a pier. It was a small private pier with a motorboat tied up near the end.

When Harry was close enough for the dory's momentum to carry it on in, he dropped the rope and landed on the pier. By flopping down onto his stomach, he was

able to reach down and guide the boat to a gentle stop. Then he lifted the kids out and put them on the dock.

The littlest one was a baby girl, with wet curls hanging across her face. She had quit crying, but she looked sort of dazed, as if she didn't know what was going on.

When Harry put the boy down on the pier beside his sister, the boy held out his hand and said, "Thank you, Mr. Angel, for saving us." Harry shook hands gravely and took off as soon as he had got the two of them started down the pier towards a brightly lighted house. It was bad enough to be seen by kids, but there was just a chance that Mr. Mazzeeck's bosses wouldn't consider it "public notice" unless grownups saw him, too. Just to make sure everything was all right, though, he circled back over the house the kids were heading for. He came down on the ridge of the roof and crawled to the edge on his hands and knees. Just as he got to the edge, he heard a woman saying, "Why you poor little darlings. Call the police, Herbert, immediately. No, no. Call the hospital. No, don't do that, we'll call their parents first. Well, don't just stand here, Herbert, do something!"

Anyway, it sounded as if something was going to get done eventually without any more help from Harry, so he headed for home.

The Leotard Mystery

The next morning when Harry picked up *The Chronicle*, the first thing he saw was a story headline reading "Tots Adrift on Bay." His heart sank. It looked like "public notice" this time for sure. But as his eyes skimmed down the column, to his surprise, he found no mention of an angel or a flying boy at all. He went back and began to read more carefully.

The little boy's name was Tommy Gibson and he was five years old, and his little sister was three. While their mother was busy making dinner they had gone out to play and climbed into the little boat that a neighbor had beached near their home. Tommy had had one rowing lesson from his father and thought he knew how to take his sister for a ride. But once in the boat, he had found it was harder than he thought it would be, and after a while he had lost one oar. Darkness had fallen, and with it came the fog before the searchers had even noticed the absence of the tiny boat and begun an almost hopeless search of the huge fog-bound bay. And then, four hours later and almost three miles from home, something—perhaps the tide, or Tommy's one oar—had brought the little boat to a dock owned by a Mr. and Mrs. Herbert Henderson, who had heard about the missing children on the radio and had notified the children's frantic parents.

Tommy and Donna were in the hospital recovering from exposure and exhaustion, but they were both going to be all right. There was a big picture of Tommy smiling from his hospital bed. He was even cuter looking than Harry remembered, with big dark eyes and a cocky grin.

It wasn't until the very last paragraph that Harry read:

> After reaching safety, Tommy refused to take any credit and insisted that he and his sister had been brought to shore by an angel. Doctor Grant attributed Tommy's angel to delirium brought on by exhaustion, but Tommy's mother had another explanation. "Tommy has always been a very imaginative child," Mrs. Gibson stated.

When Harry read that he slammed the paper down on the table. "How do you like that!" he said right out loud. Delirium! Imagination! It just went to show that grownups ought to pay more attention to what their kids said. Of course, it was a good thing for Harry that nobody had listened to Tommy's story. Still, it seemed too bad that no one would believe the poor kid. Harry hoped that somebody had the good sense to pretend at least that he thought Tommy was telling the truth. It was just like Lee said, "A little more believing would do the world a lot of good."

Thinking about Lee reminded Harry of the Plan and how long it had been since he'd worked on it. He decided to really make an effort the next week end when Mr. Brighton was home. So on Sunday afternoon he cleverly got Mr. Brighton into the kitchen by asking to hear about how he used to play football for UCLA. Sure enough, Mom sat down to listen, too, and when Mr. Brighton began to run out of stories, Harry excused himself and went out, leaving them sitting cozily side by side. He stayed away a nice long time, but what he saw when he came back was very discouraging. There was Mr. Brighton, almost upside down in the old washing machine, which had been acting up again lately, and Mom was running back and forth bringing him wrenches and things. It wasn't a very romantic scene.

It was a few days after that that Harry had another close call with the "public notice" business. It happened one night when he arrived home a little later than usual. It was a clear night and he had flown down along the coast all the way to Half Moon Bay and back.

As he came in over Kerry Street he decided it was too clear to risk a landing on the carriage house, so he came down on Madelaine's roof. He made a good quiet landing and tiptoed to the front of the building to make sure the coast was clear before he crossed the alley to his back door.

He was just peeking cautiously over the edge of the building when a car pulled to a stop almost directly below him. A man got out of the old dark-colored sedan, carrying some sort of a bundle. He stopped for a minute to whisper to the driver, who was still at the wheel of the car. Then he walked quickly to the narrow alley that separated the cleaner-ballet building from Wong's Grocery.

Harry couldn't think of any good reason why a guy would be going down that alley at that hour of the night, so he ducked under the clothesline and crept over to the other side of the roof to take a look. He reached the side of the building and peeked over in time to see the man take something out of the bundle and start to work on the back door of the Wongs' store.

It took Harry a minute or two to make himself believe that he was really seeing what he thought he was seeing. It just didn't seem possible that anyone would want to rob the Wongs. But then, all of a sudden, he remembered a rumor he'd heard about how old Mr. Williamson Wong didn't believe in banks and kept all his life-savings in a safe in the back of his store. Harry had even seen the safe when he and Mike were playing hide-and-go-seek in the big storeroom at the back.

It made Harry so mad to think that anyone would be mean enough to steal the life-savings of two nice old people like the Wongs that he almost flew right down on top of the guy. But on second thought, he realized that it wouldn't help the Wongs any for him to get himself shot, or maybe hit over the head with a crowbar. He'd be a lot smarter to go for help—and as quickly as he could.

He scooted back across the roof and down the fire

escape. Once inside the back door, it was only a few steps to the kitchen phone.

The policeman at the other end of the wire sounded awfully calm about the whole thing, as if he didn't really think Harry knew what he was talking about. He took the address of the Wongs' store, but then he said, "We'll have to have your name, sir."

The "public notice" problem flashed through Harry's mind; he made a mental grab for a substitute name and stammered out the first thing he came up with. "Mazzeeck," he said. "Mr. Tarzack Mazzeeck." He only used Mr. Mazzeeck's name because it was the first thing that came to his mind, but afterwards he decided it wasn't a bad choice. After all, if Mr. Mazzeeck wasn't planning to come back to San Francisco for over a hundred years, he ought not to mind if the San Francisco police looked for him for a few days.

As soon as he finished phoning, Harry went out on the back steps and stood there listening. Every minute he expected to hear the sound of shots coming from the direction of the store. But for a long tense time, he heard nothing at all. Finally he couldn't stand it any longer. He just had to know what was happening. He had always considered a back yard take-off too risky, but this time he took a chance. A few quick hard strokes of his wings took him to the roof of the cleaner-ballet building, and once there he dashed silently to the other side, ducking the T.V. antenna and crawling under the clothesline on the way.

In the alley below all was dark and quiet. No light or sound came from the Wongs' building. Harry looked and listened until his eyes felt bulgy and his ears were deafened by the beat of his own heart. Then, at last, something moved.

Silently a dark shadow emerged from the Wongs' storeroom door. Slowly and cautiously, the robber closed the door behind him and began to creep back up the alley. Frozen with horror, Harry watched him go. There had been no sign of the police, and in just a moment the thief would round the corner, jump into the car, and be gone. And gone, too, would be all the money the Wongs had been saving for years and years, to take care of their old age.

Afterwards Harry didn't even remember taking off, but suddenly he was in the middle of a long fast glide, heading right for the robber, who had almost reached the front of the alley. In the half-second before Harry caught up with the tiptoeing crook, it suddenly occurred to him that he didn't have the slightest idea what he was going to do once he got there. It was that unnerving thought that set off a chain reaction.

First, Harry decided against the whole thing and started to pull up; then he changed his mind and decided to go through with it. Next he frantically decided to pull up again—and right about then, he saw it was too late.

By that time, Harry's long smooth glide had turned into a waving, grabbing, flopping tumble of arms, legs and wings; and that was the mess that hit the robber squarely in the middle of his back. It knocked the wind completely out of both of them. It was Harry, however, who got his breath back first. Maybe that was because he was so used to having the wind knocked out of him,

or maybe it was just because he was on top. Anyway, after a while, Harry sat up on the robber's back and looked around.

There was still no sign of the police. There was also no sign that the crook's helper in the car had heard the commotion or was coming to investigate. Just then the guy under Harry started to wiggle.

From long experience with such things on T.V. shows, Harry knew there were two things he could do. One, he could tie the robber up; and two, he could knock him out again. Harry quickly decided on the tieing up method, except, of course, he had no rope. That was when he thought of Madelaine's clothesline.

Quick as anything, Harry bounced once on the robber, to hold him for just a minute longer, and then took off for the roof. He lit neatly, right beside the clothesline, but then he ran into trouble. The knots that held the clothesline rope to the poles were old and hard as iron. Harry could see at a glance that without a knife it was hopeless.

But right at that moment he noticed that a piece of clothing had been left hanging on the line. There was no time to be choosy, so he grabbed it, and a second later was back in the alley beside the robber who was beginning to wiggle again and gasp for breath.

The cloth was thin and stretchy and worked almost as well as a rope. One end tied the thief's hands behind his back and the other end reached clear down to bind his feet together. Harry was just pulling the last knot tight, when he heard the far-off wail of approaching sirens. The police were finally on their way.

The next day everyone on Kerry Street was talking about the attempted burglary. All up and down the street people were saying, "Have you heard this?" and "Have you heard that?" and "You know what I think," and "How do you suppose?"; but nobody bothered to ask Harry any questions at all.

Harry had managed to get back to his room and get his wings off and his pajamas on, before all the excitement began. Then when everyone started getting up to see what was going on, he straggled downstairs with the rest, trying to look sleepy and confused. So it never occurred to anyone to ask Harry what he thought about anything.

Two policemen came to the door the next morning and asked for Mr. Mazzeeck, but Mom told them that although a man by that name had been a guest there early in June, she hadn't seen him since. Mom told the police the only thing she could think of was that Mr. Mazzeeck had just happened to be back in the neighborhood and had just happened to witness the robbery. The police didn't seem to go for all those "just happeneds" very much, but it didn't look as if they had any better ideas.

One of the policemen asked Mom if she thought this Mr. Mazzeeck could have "just happened" to catch the thief and tie him up before he went on his way. Mom said that it didn't seem to her that Mr. Mazzeeck was at all the type to tackle a big strong criminal and overpower him, but that you never could tell what people would do in an emergency. The policeman seemed to agree with that, and so did Harry.

Just by keeping his mouth shut and listening, Harry found out all the things he wanted to know. Mr. Wong's money had been saved, and the robber accomplice who had waited in the car had been caught, too. The police had seen him driving away and had followed. After a block or two, he'd missed a turn and crashed into a mail-box. Then the police had come back and found the first bandit still tied up in the alley. The tied-up robber hadn't been any help at all in solving the mystery of who had captured him. All he would tell the police was that he had been hit from behind by a whole gang of people.

Harry was still keeping his mouth shut and listening the next day when Madelaine came over to gossip with Mom. Mom was working at the sink and Madelaine was sitting at the kitchen table drinking coffee. She was wearing a gunny-sack material skirt over black leotards that came clear down to her wrists and feet, a lot of necklaces made out of sea shells, and her usual long skinny ponytail. She was so excited that she wasn't using her French accent at all. Harry was listening from the other end of the table.

"And I feel almost certain, Lorna, that those police-men suspect me of knowing more than I'm telling," Madelaine said. "But believe me, I'm just as bewildered as everybody else. And believe me, Lorna, I'd be only too willing to take an oath that I don't know any more than—than Harry, here—about how that crook happened to be tied up in my new pink leotards."

And Now for Olive

It was early in August when Harry noticed that the ointment in his little silver bottle was really getting lower.
The realization came as a shock. Before that time he
had never thought about the possibility of using up the
ointment and coming to the end of everything. After
all, since the ointment was certainly magic, why couldn't
it be magic enough to fill itself up each time it was used?
But it was definitely beginning to look as if that weren't
going to happen.

Harry didn't even want to think about what it
would be like to have it over with. Speed and height and
power and the endless freedom of the night sky had
become so much a part of his life that it seemed impossible that some day he would have to give them up. But
there wasn't a thing he could do about it.

He did start trying to be more careful about the
way he poured the ointment onto his shoulders each
night, but no matter how carefully he tipped the bottle,
the glowing tear-shaped drops seemed to be always exactly the same size. So Harry decided not to worry about
it and enjoy it while it lasted. After all, magic is magic,

and there isn't any more use trying to control it to suit yourself than there is in trying to explain it.

And even if he did have to give it up in the end, Harry knew he would always be grateful for having had it. He would be grateful to Mr. Mazzeeck, and to the old Swami who made the prophecy. And he was grateful to Dad, too. Magic is the kind of thing that has to be wanted in a really special way, and it was Dad who had wanted magic for Harry more than anything.

There were some other people who would have been grateful to Mr. Mazzeeck, too, except they would never know about him. It was too bad, really, that the Wongs, for instance, would never know what Mr. Mazzeeck had done for them by giving Harry wings. And Tommy and Donna Gibson and their parents would never know either. And maybe that man in the park, too.

It was toward the middle of August that Harry found out about someone else who had a reason to be grateful to Mr. Mazzeeck. He found out one day when Lee Furdell called to him while he was out emptying wastepaper baskets.

"If you've finished your chores," Lee said, "why don't you come over for a few minutes. We haven't had a good talk for weeks." So Harry went on over. But instead of sitting somewhere in the back yard as they usually did, Lee led him right on into the house.

In all the years that Harry and Lee had been friends, this was the first time Harry had been inside the Furdells' house. He couldn't help feeling nervous as Lee put some cookies and milk out on the kitchen table and pulled up some chairs. There'd been some neighborhood talk about Olive Furdell lately, about how she was an awful lot friendlier than she used to be—and, of course, Harry remembered the time she'd brought out the divinity. But still, having cookies and milk right in Olive Furdell's own kitchen just didn't seem like a very safe thing to do.

Of course, you can't just say to someone that you're afraid of his wife, even if he already knows it, so Harry just said, "It's pretty nice outside today. Why don't we take the cookies out and eat them on the back steps?"

Lee only smiled his gentle smile. "Sit down, Harry," he said. "It's all right."

So they ate the cookies and chatted for a while and Lee told Harry about a new kind of kite he'd read about and asked how the Marriage Plan for Mom was coming along. He said he'd noticed that Clarissa Clyde was still around and he still thought that Harry ought to try to convince her that Marco's was haunted. They were trying to think of a way to haunt Clarissa without scaring out all the other boarders, when all of a sudden Olive walked in.

Harry froze in mid-sentence, but Olive only pulled out a chair and sat down and smiled at them. "Well good morning, Harry," she said. "It's nice to see you." And then she asked, "And how is your mother?" and "What are you doing this summer?" and some more of the ready-made kind of questions always asked by people who feel uncomfortable talking to kids. But the amazing thing was that you could tell she was really trying to be friendly and interested.

So the three of them sat there making stiff polite

conversation about the weather and the news in the paper and things like that. Finally, Olive said she had to get back to the shop because she was breaking in a new counter girl who might need some help. After she'd gone, Lee and Harry just sat for a while staring at their cookies.

Harry had never felt embarrassed with Lee before. With Lee you could always say whatever you felt like saying and it was always all right. But what Harry felt like saying right then just didn't seem polite, somehow. What he really wanted to say was, "Well, for Pete Squeaks! What's got into her?"

But at last Lee broke the ice. "Perhaps you've noticed that Mrs. Furdell seems a bit different lately?"

You're telling me! Harry thought, but he actually only nodded his head.

"You're not the only one to notice," Lee said. "Several people have mentioned it to me. Hadn't you heard about it before?"

"Well, yes," Harry had to admit. "You know how the people on Kerry Street like to talk about each other. But I just didn't . . . I mean I wasn't . . ."

"It *is* hard to understand," Lee went on. "You can't blame people for being puzzled. But it really isn't so much a complete change as they seem to think. Olive used to be much as she is now; but that was a long time ago. No one remembers except me." Lee sat silently, fingering his glass of milk, and then he went on. "There were hard years of sorrow and disappointment, and Olive slowly changed to . . . well, to the way you've always known her. And it wasn't all her fault, Harry."

"Well, anyway, I think it's great," Harry said. "Why everyone is saying how nice and friendly Mrs. Furdell is now, and . . ."

"Yes," Lee said. "I suppose there is bound to be a lot of talk, and there'd be even more if they knew . . ."

"If they knew . . ." Harry prompted.

Lee didn't answer right away. At last he said, "I don't know why I want to tell you this, I don't know another living soul I'd feel free to discuss it with. But I know you won't repeat it. The truth of the matter is that Olive's personality change didn't just happen. That is, there was something definite that caused it. Olive thinks she . . . that is, Olive has seen a vision."

"A v-vision?" Harry stammered.

"Yes," Lee said. "She didn't tell me about it until just a few days ago, but apparently it's been going on for quite a long time. She says she felt that one does not see a vision without a reason. And in trying to understand the reason why *she* should see an angel, she realized for the first time, what she had allowed herself to become."

Harry had almost stopped listening, except for one word that all of a sudden was ricocheting around in his head like an echo gone crazy.

"An ANGEL!" he said. "Where? When?"

"Right in our own yard," Lee said. "On the roof of the carriage house. She says she has seen it many times."

They sat a while in silence. Lee was smiling and seemed to be thinking of something pleasant, but Harry was stunned.

At last Harry said, "Maybe I ought to . . . That is,

there's something I should tell you."

But Lee held up his hand. "Excuse me for inter-rupting you, Harry, but before we change the subject, there's one more thing I want to say. Olive and I are much happier than we've been in years, and I have a feeling that you will understand when I tell you that I believe in Olive's angel. I believe in Olive's angel and I *want* to believe in it."

Harry shut up.

A Mummy from Mars

The day after Harry and Lee talked about Olive's angel, Harry had a very bright idea. He had been thinking about how he had used his wings to help several other people, even when he didn't know he was helping, and it occurred to him that he might use them to solve his own problems. And right then, Harry's biggest problem —besides his clumsiness, which was pretty hopeless—was how to get rid of Miss Clyde and get Mom and Mr. Brighton to marry each other.

Putting the idea of using his wings together with Lee's idea of haunting Miss Clyde, Harry came up with a terrific scheme. If he could make Olive Furdell think he was an angel without even trying, why couldn't he, with a little effort, make Clarissa think he was something scarier. The biggest problem was making sure no one saw him except Clarissa, but Harry soon thought of a way to do that.

That afternoon he spent some time rummaging around in the attic for something he remembered putting there after last Halloween. After a while he found it in a box of other holiday junk. It was a mask. One of those gruesome rubber ones that pull on over your head. It was one of those monster faces with scars and warts and fangs all over the place.

Harry's plan was to wait for an extra dark or foggy night and then fly around to Clarissa's window and knock on it. She wouldn't be able to see much except the mask and the fact that it was floating in the air two stories above the ground. That ought to be enough to scare anybody into moving.

It was a typical San Francisco August, foggy almost every night, so Harry didn't have long to wait. That very night, when he looked out of his bedroom window, the damp gray mist was so thick he couldn't even make out the T.V. antenna on Madelaine's roof. So instead of going to bed or out on a flight, Harry just waited. He sat on the stairs between the second and third floor until he heard Clarissa Clyde come up to her bedroom. Then he went back to his room and got ready.

It's not a bit easy to see in a thick fog with a rubber mask over your whole head, and Harry came close to bumping into the chimney as he flew over the top of the house. It would have been his first bruise in a long time. But, fortunately, he just missed, and he made it over and down to Clarissa's window without any more trouble.

The window shade was down so Harry didn't have to worry about being seen before he was ready. He eased up to the window and rested his hands on the outside sill. By hanging on tightly and keeping his wings going gently, he was able to keep his head with its monster face on a level with the window. When he was all set he knocked sharply on the glass.

For a second nothing happened, and then the shade
was drawn quickly to one side, and—to Harry's horror—
there was another monster looking right back at him. It
was so awful-looking that Harry forgot about hanging on
to the window sill, and before he remembered to get his
wings going, he had dropped down several feet. If he
hadn't been so experienced at flying, he might have had
a serious accident. But he caught himself in time and
flew quickly back around the house and scrambled in his
own window. Then he sat on his bed in the dark and
shivered.

But even after his heart began to slow down and he

was able to think more calmly, he still couldn't imagine what it was he had seen. It couldn't have been his own reflection in the glass of the window, because it wasn't the same kind of monster at all. The one Harry had seen was more like a mummy. There had been a white bandage thing around the chin and the skin was all caked and cracked as if it were covered with layers of clay. Only on top of its head were a lot of round disk-like objects, like maybe it was some kind of mechanized thing from Mars. "A mummy from Mars," Harry was saying to himself with a shaky grin, when all of a sudden he became aware of a commotion going on downstairs. He had a feeling that he'd been hearing it for quite a while, but he'd been too busy thinking about the mummy to pay any attention.

Somebody was yelling down on the second floor, and Harry could hear doors slamming and people running around. With all that noise going on, Harry realized he'd have to go downstairs, or Mom would be sure to come up to see why he hadn't. He leaped off the bed and recited the reverse incantation.

A few minutes later, when Harry, dressed now in his robe and pajamas, started down to the second floor, the screaming had stopped. When he reached the hall, Mr. Konkel, Mrs. Pusey and a traveling salesman named Mr. Lewis, were talking together at one end of the hall, and at the other end Mr. Brighton was apparently having a spell of silent hysterics. Mom and Clarissa were no place to be seen.

When Mr. Brighton saw Harry, he stopped laughing enough to motion Harry to come downstairs with him. "What happened?" Harry asked. "What's all the yelling about?" But Mr. Brighton only put his finger to his still laughing mouth and went on leading the way to the kitchen.

When Mr. Brighton had poured himself some coffee, he finally stopped laughing and started explaining. "It was Miss Clyde," he said. "A few minutes ago she came running out into the hall insisting she'd seen some sort of terrible-looking face at her window. Your mother's in her room with her now trying to calm her down."

"Well for Pete Squeaks!" Harry said as innocently as he could. "What do you suppose she saw?"

Mr. Brighton started to laugh again. "I don't know," he said. "But judging by the fact that her window is at least twenty feet above the ground, and by certain other observations, I'd say she probably got a glimpse of her own reflection."

Just about then Mom came in and sat down with them, and the three of them sat there and laughed the way they'd done the night Miss Thurgood sat in the water heater flood. Only this time Harry still wasn't quite sure just what he was laughing about. At least he wasn't sure until Mom started describing what Clarissa had looked like when she ran out into the hall screaming that a ghost had looked in her window.

Mom said that Clarissa had been wearing a mud pack, and a thing called a chin strap that was supposed to get rid of double chins, plus a bunch of big fat hair curlers. It wasn't until he heard Mom's description that Harry was completely convinced that he hadn't really seen a mummy from Mars after all.

Eavesdropping — The Hard Way

The haunting scheme worked just the way it was supposed to. The very next day Miss Clarissa Clyde packed up her imitation alligator bags and went away. But even though that was what he'd been hoping for, Harry didn't feel altogether happy about it in the days that followed.

In the first place, he couldn't help feeling a bit guilty. Scaring someone just a little to get her to move was one thing, but Harry had a notion that Miss Clyde hadn't left just because she was scared. It's almost fun sometimes, after it's all over, to look back on a good scare, especially if it's the kind of thing that makes a good story to tell your friends. But nobody tells his friends about being embarrassed in front of a lot of other people. Harry couldn't help feeling a little mean every time he thought about poor Miss Clyde running out there in front of the other boarders in all her beauty stuff. He really hadn't meant it to work that way.

In the second place, the whole thing began to look like a lot of wasted effort. Even without Clarissa around, Mom and Mr. Brighton didn't seem to be getting anywhere. They did spend a little more time talking to each other; but as far as Harry could tell, it was all friendly public sort of conversation, in front of everybody. And from what Harry had observed about such things, they weren't going to make any progress at all that way.

By the end of August Harry was feeling really gloomy. Not only was the Plan a failure, but as far as he could tell by looking in the bottle, he had only about enough magic ointment left for one more flight. In fact, he didn't fly for several nights, partly because he was saving that last flight for a special occasion, and party because he just couldn't bear to use it up and then face the fact that his wings were gone forever. His wings gone, the summer almost over, and nothing to look forward to but lonely old Kerry Street, with no kids to fool around with and nothing to do.

It was on the very last day of August that Harry walked down to Wong's Grocery after dinner to chat with the Wongs and see if they knew when Mike might be coming back from the Sierras. While they were talking, he got started helping Mr. Wong stock the can shelves, and by the time they were finished it was already dark. When Harry finally got back to Marco's, Mrs. Pusey and Mr. Konkel were in the living room, but he didn't see Mom or Mr. Brighton anywhere. He went on out to the kitchen, but they weren't there either. At last, he went back to the front room and asked Mrs. Pusey where Mom was. Just as calm as could be Mrs. Pusey said, "I believe your mother and Mr. Brighton are out on the veranda."

Sure enough, from the dining room bay window, Harry could get a glimpse of them, sitting side by side on the porch swing, talking and laughing. But no matter how hard he stretched his ears, he couldn't quite hear what they were saying. Just the same, as he went on up to his room, he was feeling pretty excited and hopeful.

It was after he got to his room that he had another bright idea. At least it seemed like a good one at the time. Since he was going to have to use the last drops of magic ointment sometime, he might as well do it tonight. He'd get all ready and then he'd begin his final flight with a little detour. He'd just light for a moment on the roof of the veranda and check on the conversation going on below. After all, it wouldn't be just ordinary eavesdropping because he sort of had a right to know. Then he would go on from there and have a wonderful extra-long flight.

It wasn't many minutes later that Harry eased out of his window, coasted silently around the house, and came to a stop at the opposite end of the veranda roof from where Mom and Mr. Brighton were sitting. He didn't dare land directly over the swing because even when you're a very experienced flier, you sometimes make a bit of a thud when you land.

He came down nicely and began to move quietly along the roof. He had almost reached the point he was headed for when he was betrayed by a smooth-worn gym shoe and a dew-wet shingle. Right over Mom and Mr. Brighton's heads, Harry sat down with a shattering thump.

He slid over on to his stomach and lay there listening. Below him he heard Mom say, "For heaven's sake! What was that?"

"It sounded as if something heavy lit on the roof," Mr. Brighton said. "I'll take a look."

Footsteps crossed the veranda to the front steps, and Harry panicked. If Mr. Brighton walked out a little distance from the house, he would be able to see the entire veranda roof, and it would be impossible for Harry to get to his feet, take off, and be out of sight in time to avoid being seen.

There was only one thing to do. It might not get Harry out of trouble, but at least there'd be no "public notice" and Mr. Mazzeeck wouldn't be in dutch with his company. Lying right there on his stomach, Harry quickly recited the reverse incantation.

Dream of the earthbound—Spin and Flow
Flicker and Fold and Furl and NO!

Just as always, there was the tingling, shrinking sensation, and the whirling dizziness. It was the dizziness that Harry had forgotten to take into account. It must have been the spinning dark clouds in his mind that made him loosen his grip on the slippery shingles. But whatever it was, the next thing Harry knew, he was coming to on the bed in Mom's room and a strange man was bending over him. Mom and Mr. Brighton were standing at the foot of the bed.

"Well, young man," the doctor said. "I hope you've learned a lesson about playing games on the roof in the dark. You're pretty lucky you didn't break an arm or leg." He turned to Mom, "I can't find a thing wrong with him except a few bruises and a small bump on the head. But you might keep an eye on him for a few hours, and it wouldn't be a bad idea to take him to his regular doctor tomorrow for a check-up."

After the doctor left, Mom and Mr. Brighton came back and the three of them had a talk. When it was over, Mom and Mr. Brighton seemed to be satisfied with Harry's explanation of how it had happened, but Harry wasn't. It made him feel pretty bad to think they would believe he was dumb enough to dress up in a pair of Mom's drapes and prance around on the roof playing Superman.

After Mr. Brighton left, Harry got sleepy and wanted to go on up to his own room, but Mom told him to go to sleep right where he was. She said she was comfortable where she was on the chaise longue and she wanted to stay there a while longer anyway. Harry knew she was keeping an eye on him like the doctor said, and there was no use arguing with Mom about a thing like that.

When Harry woke up sometime later, he had been dreaming that he heard someone crying. The room was dimly lighted. Just as Harry opened his eyes, the hall door opened and Mr. Brighton came in carrying two cups of coffee. "I brought up a little coffee," he whispered. "Why, Lorna, you are crying? What is it? Is Harry worse?"

"No-o-o." Mom's voice was trembly. "He's asleep, and he seems to be fine. It isn't that."

"Then what is it? It must be something serious, to make you cry."

"Well, it is about Harry in a way," Mom said. "You

know what he's always been like. I've been so happy and proud of the way he was turning out, even without a father to help him. But something has been wrong this summer. His mind seems to be a million miles away, and he's so sleepy and groggy acting. He hasn't wanted to do anything or go anywhere all summer, and he doesn't seem to have any of his normal interests. I feel as if it's my fault for disappointing him again about the summer trip he wanted to take. And now this strange thing to-night. It just doesn't seem like Harry at all."

"Lorna," Mr. Brighton said, "I don't think you have a thing to worry about. A kid like Harry doesn't change overnight. If there's anything strange about Harry this summer, it's probably only that he's growing so fast it's worn him all out."

Mr. Brighton set the coffee down, pulled up the vanity bench, and sat down. But Mom went on sniffing and gulping and holding her handkerchief over her eyes. "Look here, Lorna," Mr. Brighton said after a while, "if there *is* any thing wrong with Harry—and mind you, I'm not saying there is—but if you've even a suspicion there might be, I think I know just the thing to straighten him out." In the dim light it was hard to tell for sure, but Harry thought Mr. Brighton was grinning. His voice had that sort of sound to it.

"Yes?" Mom said, lifting her head a little.

"Well, it's just one man's opinion, of course, but it seems to me that the best thing in the world for Harry would be a good stepfather."

"Oh, Hal," Mom said, shaking her head but with a smile in her voice. "You're awful. Can't you be serious about anything? I'm really worried."

"I am serious," Mr. Brighton said. "Look. I'm solemn as a judge."

"All right, then. You're serious," Mom said. She sounded just a little bit sarcastic. "And I suppose you have someone in particular in mind for the job. Mr. Konkel, maybe. He'd be a fine one."

"No, not exactly," Mr. Brighton said, "I've been seriously considering applying for the job myself."

"Hal!" Mom said in a weak little voice, but Harry wasn't so bashful.

He sat right up in bed and yelled, "Whoopee!"

Good-by Magic —
Good-by Black and Blue

The next morning Harry woke up to a curious mixture of feelings. First of all, he thought about Mom and Mr. Brighton (or Mom and Hal, he should say—that's what Mr. Brighton had said to call him, for the present at least. Thinking about Mom and Hal and the farm in Marin and everything made Harry feel so great that he bounced out of bed. And that made him feel awful—at least physically.

That fall off the roof last night must have really been something. Harry had been stiff and sore before, but this was something else again. It felt as if nearly every bone in his body was protesting, and there was still a big bump on the back of his head. Exploring with his finger tips, he decided that his whole back was just one king-sized bruise. Harry sat back carefully on the edge of the bed.

Sitting there, thinking and rubbing the bump on his head, Harry remembered about the magic ointment and that made him feel bad, mentally, too. Boy! Wasn't that just like him? Falling off the roof and spoiling his chances for one last wonderful flight. But after a few minutes of gloom, he decided he might as well knock it off. After all, there was a lot to be happy about. And who knows? Maybe there was still enough ointment left for one more flight. He'd been in such a hurry to get started last night, he hadn't checked very carefully. At least, it would be worth a try.

Harry eased himself up enough to reach over to the silver bottle, removed the cork, and peered inside. The bottom seemed to be covered with a thin film. It just might be enough for one more flight. With that thought, Harry hobbled downstairs to find Mom and ask a few questions.

Mom was busy in the kitchen so Harry poured himself a big glass of orange juice and got comfortably settled at the table to wait until she was able to stay in one

place long enough to do some answering. Mom was bustling around getting breakfast and humming little bits of tunes under her breath. Harry noticed that for the first time in a long while she didn't look the least bit tired.

When Mom had finished mixing the muffins and had them in the oven, she sat down for a minute with a cup of coffee and Harry got his chance. He found out that the wedding was set for the end of September, and they'd be moving to the farmhouse in Marin just as soon after that as the tenants could find a new place to live.

"There's another thing I'd like to know," Harry said. "If Hal has been wanting to get up his nerve to ask you to marry him for so long, how come he spent so much time talking to that Miss Clyde?"

Mom laughed. "Well, you have to admit he didn't have much choice. Clarissa is the kind who's pretty hard to avoid, at least without being rude."

"Yeah, I guess so." Harry said. "And another thing. How come you were being so friendly to Mr. Konkel? That really had me worried."

Mom laughed, but then she looked down at her coffee and her cheeks got pink. "I'm ashamed to admit it, but I guess I was just trying to convince everybody, myself included, that I didn't care about Hal and Clarissa." Mom stopped and thought for a moment and then she went on. "You see, Harry, you don't know all there is to know about this whole thing. Some time ago, not too long after Hal first came to board with us he . . . well, he seemed interested in marrying me. I discouraged him so completely that he thought I wouldn't ever change my mind. I did change my mind, but he didn't know it—at least, not until last night."

"Well, for Pete Squeaks!" Harry said. And here he'd been so darn sure that he always knew when any romantic stuff was going on in the boarding house. He'd sure been fooled this time. He had to think about that for a minute before he got around to asking, "What did you want to go and do that for? Discourage him, I mean?"

Mom shrugged, "There were a lot of reasons. I'd made up my mind a long time ago that I wasn't ever going to get married again. And I was worried about how you would react to having a stepfather. But mostly, I just hadn't gotten to know Hal well enough."

Harry was just having a few quiet thoughts about how it was true, all right, about women not being able to make up their minds, when he remembered that it had taken him quite a while to make up his mind that he'd like having Hal as a stepfather. So, maybe it was only natural for Mom to take a long time to decide on him for a husband. He was just getting ready to tell Mom that he understood about her being so wishy-washy about the whole thing, when she interrupted.

"Well anyway, Harry, I guess you know that we have you to thank for getting things straightened out. If it hadn't been for your silly tumble off the roof, Hal might not have asked me. He'd about decided that we Marcos didn't need or want anyone to look out for us; but last night—with all the bruises and tears—it was pretty plain he'd been wrong about that. So he decided the time had come."

That made Harry feel a lot better. He hadn't really wasted those last drops of ointment, after all. Maybe he hadn't had a last long flight, but it looked like—entirely by accident—those drops had brought him something even more important. "And I *do* mean 'by accident,'" Harry thought, gingerly rubbing the bump on the back of his head.

That afternoon Mom took Harry to see their family doctor, as the emergency doctor had recommended. Dr. Kimura had taken care of Harry since he'd first come back to San Francisco when he was just a little kid. Dr. Kimura was a great kidder and, sure enough, he had quite a bit to say about a boy Harry's age who didn't know any better than to play games on the roof. As a rule Harry didn't mind a little kidding, but this time he couldn't help wishing that the doctor would knock it off. He was getting a little bit mad when Dr. Kimura said something that made up for all the teasing.

The doctor was examining Harry's back when all of a sudden he said, "Well, well, well."

"What is it Doctor? Is anything wrong?" Mom asked.

"Wrong?" the doctor said. "Oh, no. These bruises aren't anything to worry about. In fact, I consider a few bruises standard equipment for a boy Harry's age. I was just being impressed by the way Harry's been growing up since he was last in. Just look at those shoulders, Mrs. Marco."

"Yes, I'd noticed lately how his shoulders were filling out," Mom said.

"Yes, sir!" Dr. Kimura said, clapping Harry on one

of the biggest bruises, "that's quite a change for such a short time. What have you been up to this summer? Weight lifting?" Of course, Harry wasn't about to tell him what he'd really been doing, but before he had to try to think something up, the doctor went on. "Yes indeed, that looks to me like the beginning of a real athlete's build."

After that, it wasn't a bit hard for Harry to forgive him for all the kidding.

By the next evening most of the stiffness was gone from his back and Harry decided to find out for sure if there was enough ointment left for one last flight. There was that slight film of liquid in the bottom of the silver bottle, and it wouldn't hurt to try. As he started getting ready, Harry kept telling himself that it probably wouldn't work, so he wouldn't be too disappointed in case it didn't, but he couldn't help hoping desperately down underneath.

But when he tipped the bottle over his bare shoulders nothing at all came out. Not even when he shook it up and down, time after time. At last he put his finger up inside the bottle and ran it around the inside surface. It felt moist when he pulled it out, so he quickly rubbed it on one shoulder. He did the same thing to the other shoulder and then he closed his eyes and recited the incantation.

Wing feather, bat leather, hollow bone,
Gift of Icarus and Oberon,
Dream of the earthbound—Spin and Flow
Fledge and Flutter and Fan and GO!

There was a tiny tingle, a twinge, and that was all. When Harry opened his eyes and looked back over his shoulder, nothing was there. No huge white arching wings, nothing at all, except—except one big white feather, drifting very slowly down to the floor.

It was with an awful feeling of sorrow and loss, that Harry took down the shoe box that held his most important keepsakes. Just as his happiness and pride in his wings had always seemed too big for one person, the sadness he felt as he put away the bottle and feather seemed to be more than just his. He was putting the shoe box back on the highest closet shelf, when suddenly he had an idea. He took the feather out and looked at it again.

It was long and cloudy white; soft, and yet strangely strong. There was something about it so pure and perfect, you knew without a doubt, that it came from the wing of something entirely out of the ordinary. Instead of putting the feather away again with the silver bottle, Harry put it inside his shirt. Then he went over to make a social call on the Furdells.

It was just barely past dark, so the Furdells weren't surprised to see him. Besides, Harry, and other people, too, were beginning to call on the Furdells a lot, since —well—since Olive started being different. Harry sat around and chatted long enough to make it look natural, and when he left he knew where both the Furdells were and what they were doing. He knew, for instance, that they wouldn't be likely to look out the back windows for the next few minutes. As soon as he was outside, he headed for the carriage house roof.

Sure enough, the little table was still sitting against the railing at the corner of the roof. The candle was in a little lantern now, so the wind wouldn't blow it out when it was lit, and there were fresh flowers in the vase. Harry ran his hand over the softly gleaming feather for the last time. Then he tucked the end of it under the lantern so it would be sure not to blow away. After all, he had other things to remember by.

For only a moment Harry looked up into the endless open sky before he turned and hurried down the stairs and home. Back at Marco's, Mom was ironing in the kitchen and Hal was drinking coffee at the table. Harry sat down too, and it wasn't long before they were having a great conversation, all about the farm and trips they could take on Hal's vacation and things like that. After a while, Hal went upstairs to get some snapshots he wanted to show them, and Harry had a chance to ask a question that had been on his mind lately.

"Mom," he said, "do you remember the prophecy that old fortuneteller made when I was little?"

"Of course," Mom said. "I'm sure I'll never forget it. Your father talked about it so often."

"Didn't he say that I had a rare gift and I'd have a special kind of magic?"

Mom nodded.

"What do you think he meant by that?"

"I don't know, Harry. Not really. But I've always had a theory of my own about it. Of course, your father was sure it meant that you would grow up to be a very famous magician, but I . . . well, I always thought it might be referring to something else."

"What?" Harry asked. "What did you think it meant?"

Mom stopped ironing and sat down at the table with her chin on her hand. She thought a while before she said, "I don't know if I can explain it very well, but it's something like this. It seems to me we all have a little magic. It's as if life makes a magic circle around each of us, but its size is entirely up to you. If you try to make your circle closed and exclusively yours, it never grows very much. There are even people who try to make their magic so private and tight that eventually it almost strangles them. Only a circle that has lots of room for anybody who needs it, has enough spare space to hold any real magic. Does that make any sense to you?"

"I think so," Harry said. "But I don't really see what it has to do with me and the prophecy."

"Well, it's just that you've been crowding people into your circle ever since you were a tiny boy. That seems like a rare gift to me. I've always thought there was going to be room in your life for all sorts of people —and all kinds of magic, too."

Mom went back to her ironing then and Harry thought about what she had said. He wasn't too sure just what she'd been trying to say, but, at least, he was glad to hear that she didn't think the prophecy meant that he ought to try to grow up to be a great stage magician. Because he had always been pretty sure he'd much rather not.

It was the next morning, the day before Labor Day, that Mike Wong came back from his summer in the Sierras. He had just two days to spend with his grandparents before school started. Of course, he came over to see Harry right away. They sat on the front steps and talked, and Mike had lots to tell about his summer in the mountains. Harry had very little to say because nothing much had happened on Kerry Street—not that he could talk about, anyway.

Mike was anxious to show Harry the new pitch he'd developed during the summer, so right after lunch they collected their baseball stuff and headed for the bus stop and Golden Gate Park.

When Harry got home from the park that night, it was almost dinner time. He stuck his head in the kitchen and yelled "Hi!" at Mom to let her know he was home, and ran upstairs. Four flights, three stairs at a step, without a stop or a stumble.

He wasn't even out of breath when he got to his room but he threw himself down on his bed anyway. He just lay there on his back for a while, thudding his fist into his mitt and grinning to himself, while he let his mind go back over the afternoon.

There'd been that long hard run to make a scooping shoestring catch of one of Mike's best hits. And then there was the way he'd clobbered half a dozen of Mike's fast balls, and even a couple of his fancy new sleeper pitches. Mike had almost gotten mad for a minute, but then he'd gotten into the spirit of the thing, and he ended up being almost as tickled as Harry was himself. "Holy Toledo, Harry," he kept on saying, "What have you been having for breakfast lately?" or "Are you sure you're the same Harry Marco I used to know?" and other remarks like that. Finally Mike said, "Pretty sneaky, I call it. Keeping all this a secret until we got to the park. Boy, if I'd improved the way you have, I'd have been bragging before you had a chance to say hello."

Harry just grinned and said, "Yeah, I'm the sneaky one, all right."

But actually, it wasn't that at all. Actually, it wasn't until that afternoon in Golden Gate Park that Harry realized what a difference a summer of flying—and growing, too—could make.

His Black and Blue Magic was over; gone with the summer. But it wasn't going to be nearly so hard to give it up now. It wasn't nearly so hard now that he was saying good-by to his everyday black and blue at the same time.

That night Harry went to bed with his mind full of great things to think about. There was moving to the country, no more worry about Mom working too hard, and how neat it would be to be one of the good athletes at his new school in Marin County. He was just at the edge of sleep, and his daydreams were getting a little mixed up with real dreams, when a face appeared in front of him. The face took shape gradually, out of a school scene Harry had been imagining. It grew plainer and clearer until it entirely blotted out the dreamed-up picture of Harry making a home run while his new classmates cheered wildly in the background.

Just about the time Harry recognized the face as Mr. Mazzeeck's, it began to change. Mr. Mazzeeck's chubby wrinkled cheeks faded and melted and flowed into a different face entirely—a thin keen face with high cheek bones beneath dark burning eyes.

The eyes seemed to be looking directly at Harry, and suddenly some words popped into his mind right out of nowhere. Some words that sounded vaguely familiar:

> Mog will not remove a curse,
> Till Better Triumphs over Worst.
> Till Bad-to-Worse
> Has been Reversed
> And out of Error—Good has Burst.

Harry was pretty sure it was the verse that Mr. Mazzeeck said explained the cure for enchantment, but the words hadn't made any sense to Harry then, and he was too tired to figure them out now. He certainly hadn't realized that he'd memorized them from reading them just that one time.

That's funny, Harry thought. He sat up and looked around expectantly, but the face was gone and everything was dark and quiet. He waited like that for quite a while, but nothing more happened, so at last Harry lay back down and finished going to sleep.